Wizards of Zannus: Quest to Rule the Realm

Tanisha Beecher Bell

Dedicated to my dear sweet Aria Renae Bell

A Special Note from the Author

Dear readers, welcome to the pages of my first fantasy fiction novel. Please note that the plot ended up being a bit more complicated than I had realized. So complicated, I almost did not publish it. So, I encourage you to always pay close attention.

I have developed a new language, the ancient tongue, that is used by some of the characters. These new words and their meanings can be found at the back of this book, though it's likely you may not need the interpretations, as the meanings are expressed to the extent possible, within context.

Additionally, for your convenience, I included the following introduction of the backdrop, as well as the names of the lead characters and their mission. You may quickly reference the introduction page as you read, should you forget whom a character is, or what he or she is trying to accomplish.

With that said, do enjoy this short and spicy masterpiece. I welcome opportunities for improvement, so please send me an email of your feedback. Tell me, should this be my last fantasy fiction? Lol! If you think my work is the bomb, then share it with everyone you know on social media.

Much love!
Tanisha

Wizards of Zannus: Quest to Rule the Realm

INTRODUCTION

A small group of planetoids that form the Zannus Realm is located a few light-years away from earth, just outside of the constellation Centaurus. Zannus Realm forms the Zannusian Pyramid, which comprises four kingdoms. Kingdoms Asteria, Svania and Octushi form the base of this pyramidal monarchy, while the fourth Kingdom, Nuria, referred to as the light of the realm, sits at the realm's apex.

Kingdom Asteria: Asterians, through their wizard's unique powers, have forced their dominance over Kingdom Nuria. For hundreds of years, the Asterians have maximized Wizard Qarhan's beaming ability to transport themselves across kingdoms to enforce their reign upon Kingdom Nuria. To date, Wizard Qarhan has been the only wizard who is powerful enough to disappear from one kingdom and reappear in another. Nurians feel urged to adhere to the laws that are enacted by Asteria's governing body and administered by the kingdom's chief and combatants through the help of Wizard Qarhan.

Kingdom Nuria: This is known as the land of light because its outer atmosphere glows similarly to the sun's corona—and is thus called light of the realm as its rays provide light and warmth for the other kingdoms. The Nurians are a people of great intellect. They possess no wizard or special power, and therefore use their vast intellect to provide a means of escaping Asteria's rule. Some believe that the Nurians' intellectual acumen may be their own special power, given their lack of a wizard. Nevertheless, intelligence officers who study celestial objects and space, teach Nurians the importance of attaining the knowledge necessary to forge their escape from Zannus Realm, and ultimately, Asteria's rule. The Nurians find it critical to hide much of their intellect from the

Asterian government, in hopes of maintaining their freedom to further their research and promote innovation—the majority of which is kept hidden from the Asterians.

Emperor Lunar, acting Chief of Kingdom Nuria, leads a team of researchers and intelligence officers in exploration of prospective new planets for their people to inhabit. Other research goals include concealment of a recently constructed spacecraft.

Additionally, intelligence officers, using modified gravitational microlensing, have discovered Planet Earth; however, a recent incident has suddenly disrupted their efforts to successfully probe earth's gases, atmospheric pressure, and temperatures. This has resulted in prioritizing the development of a new and more easily accessible means of transport, which is now underway.

Kingdom Svania, Kingdom of the Temptresses: This is a kingdom of only women. Men who happen to visit the kingdom become subdued by the essence of its all-female inhabitants. Many believe that this is the reason Asterians have not yet conquered the Svanians. Wizard Ziva has casted an intrusion spell that keeps male visitors subdued, protecting Svanian women from romantic advances of outsiders. Yet, others may say that Svanian women's striking beauty softens Asterian men's attitude towards them, resulting in a harmonious relationship between the two kingdoms.

The beautiful empress, Senya, rules Kingdom Svania alongside the very powerful wizard, Ziva. Wizard Ziva represents the human half of the kingdom's lifeforce, while the water-force which fuels the Pterion Springs, represents the remaining half.

A major difference exists between Svanian wizard, Ziva, and Asterian wizard, Qarhan. Unlike Wizard Qarhan, Ziva does not possess teleporting abilities. The powerful and devious seer, Aries, begins to question why Ziva has never beamed across kingdoms as Wizard Qarhan does. This curiosity leads Aries to set in motion a plan perilous enough to shift the sanctity of the kingdom while compromising the entire realm of Zannus.

Every seven years, a new empress is appointed by Ziva to rule the land for seven years. This appointment by Ziva is guided by the water-force. This process is key to ensuring survival of the Svanian Kingdom. Each empress is appointed seven maidens to reside with her in the Citadel during her reign. It is believed that the lifeforce reveals an enchanted fountain made visible and accessible to each goddess. Drinking from this fountain pauses aging which resumes once an empress' reign ends. The fountain is secretly referred to by each empress as the fountain of life.

Kingdom Octushi: This kingdom is rendered untenable as its chronic water shortage has resulted in an atmosphere that is extremely hostile to plant and human life. The land is dull, dry, and desolate.

Lead Characters

Asterian Leaders:

Akello___________________Chief of the Kingdom of Asteria. Akello is the successor to his indomitable father, Leo.

Leo and Wanniya_________Akello's parents. Both are Natives of Kingdom Asteria.

Councilmen______________Constitute the governmental Body of Kingdom Asteria.

Wizard Qarhan___________Wizard of the Kingdom of Asteria. Qarhan is a part of Asteria's governmental body, and serves at the pleasure of Asteria's ruler.

Svanian Leaders:

Empress Senya___________Svanian temptress and ruler. Senya's reign is overseen by Wizard Ziva, and ultimately The lifeforce of Svania.

Wizard Ziva_____________Wizard of Svania. Constitutes the human Half of Svania's lifeforce. Ziva, together with the waterforce, make up the lifeforce of Svania.

Svanian Leaders Continued

The Waterforce___________Powerful and omni-hearing second half of Svania's lifeforce. The waterforce, together with the Wizard Ziva, constitute the lifeforce of Svania.

Lifeforce___________Core of a kingdom. Made whole through forcefields, and most times sustain and tether inhabitants to their respective kingdoms.

Aries the Seer___________Regarded by her society as the wicked trickster; her gift of foresight is rare and mysterious.

Nurian Leaders:

Emperor Lunar___________Ruler of Kingdom Nuria.

Kaleb___________Lead Intelligence Officer of Kingdom Nuria.

Octushian Leader:

The Shadow___________Ominous and unbeknownst lifeforce of Octushi.

CHAPTER ONE
Kingdom Asteria

On his twenty-sixth birthday, Akello was coronated Chief of the Asterians. Leo, his father and predecessor, had dutifully led Asteria for many years, but now yielded his title, with honor, to young Akello. The entire kingdom looked forward to a younger and stronger leader, who would guide its people with great tenacity and bring greater innovation and esteem to the land. Leo looked forward to seeing his son put all the years of training to great use, making the kingdom of Asteria even more revered among all the kingdoms of Zannus Realm. Akello seemed proud of his new role as leader and already had ideas for change. For many years he's waited for the day when he'd be allowed to present his ideas before the governmental body, known as the Council.

"Congratulations, Chief!" a group of people cheered as Akello strolled by with his father, Leo.

"Thank you! It is an honor," Akello beamed, his neat locks bounced against broad shoulders that were anchored by his tall, toned body. Akello sported an all-white salwar suit.

"Son, you don't have to say it's an honor every single time," Leo's voice boomed.

"I know, father. I just can't help it. I'm excited to finally feel what it's like to walk in your shoes."

"Akello, you have been made leader, so, you should not appear weak before the people."

"Yes, father, but connecting with my people can never make me weak."

"My point is, Akello, you cannot appear to be too excited, or you'll be seen as weak."

"Father, you know that I'm strong. The Council knows this—my people know this."

"But …"

"Father, I intend to apply all the lessons you've taught me. But I also have my own ideas of the type of leader that I should be. Connecting with the kingdom is one such idea."

"I see. While we're on the subject, what other ideas do you have in mind?" Leo asked, pausing their stroll to seat himself on a large stone next to a brook.

"Well, I was saving my ideas for our meeting with the Council," Akello replied, seating himself next to Leo.

"I am the Council," Leo said, appearing slightly perturbed.

"You are only one twelfth of the governing body, father."

"How dare you reduce my title to such a trivial standing!"

"I do not wish to argue …"

"Son, I believe there are things that we need to discuss."

"What things, father?" Akello asked, looking away from his father and eying the brook instead. He was no longer enthused by the cheers from passersby. Neither was he interested in the new path the conversation had taken. He had hoped to keep his ideas from everyone, including his father, until his first presentation to the Council. Now his father sought to vet these ideas himself.

"Father, why do you insist on treating me like a child?" Akello stalled.

"Why are you stalling, Akello?" Leo persisted, folding his arms across his broad chest. Leo was both strapping and intimidating. His white kameez fluttered in the wind, scarcely hiding his sturdy built.

"The truth is, I just do not wish to share these ideas with you. Please respect my wish, father, as I am now ruler of the kingdom. Wait for the meeting—it's quickly approaching anyway."

"Very well, Chief," Leo acquiesced, standing to greet his wife as she approached them. "My beautiful Wanniya," he greeted, eyeing Wanniya's teal kaftan that accentuated her smooth caramel skin and deep brown hair. Wanniya is on the mature side of the age spectrum, with strong cheekbones, a flawless asymmetric haircut, and a youthful flare.

"You flatter me, darling," Wanniya uttered softly, kissing Leo lightly on the lips. "How are my two favorite men doing today?" She eyed Akello fondly.

"Mother, you're looking elegant as usual." Akello said, forcing a smile.

"Why must you both flatter me to hide your true feelings? What's really going on here, my darlings? What intense discussion have I intruded on?" She ran a gentle palm over Akello's cheek.

"All is well, mother. Father was just leaving and I'll remain here for just a while to admire the brook."

"Fine. Go on with your secrets. But be reminded that the truth will be revealed one way or another," Wanniya teased.

"Let's return to the sanctuary, my dear." Leo kissed her palm.

"Very tempting, but I must speak with Akello about his presentation at the upcoming meeting with the Council."

"What about my presentation, mother?" Akello sunk into his stone-seat. *Not again. Not after he'd successfully managed to quash this talk with his very persistent father.*

"Well, I planned on vetting your ideas with your father before you presented them to the Council."

Right. Here we go again. "Mother, please go ahead and take the walk with father."

"Pardon me?" Wanniya exclaimed.

"I mean, father will explain everything to you."

"Let's get going, dear, I'm afraid our son is in a terrible mood today."

"But why would he refuse your counsel when you, his own father, possess years upon years of experience in being ruler?"

"Mother, while I do respect father's experience, I choose to do this on my own."

"I see your point, and I hear you," Leo uttered, retreating. "Wanniya and I will allow you time alone to gather your thoughts and be your own man."

"Son, surely you're not rejecting your father's experienced input," Wanniya countered.

"Let us walk, my love." Leo locked arms with his wife and led her away from their sullen son.

Akello watched as his parents strolled off into the distance. He was relieved to have outmaneuvered them; though, not much time remained before his big reveal. He wished there was a way to also prepare the Council—everyone, for what he was about to propose.

"The boy is hiding something. I'm concerned—I do not trust him," Wanniya murmured.

"What sort of ideas would a new leader wish to keep hidden from being vetted?" Leo replied pensively.

CHAPTER TWO
Kingdom Svania

The Kingdom of Svania, land of the temptresses, ruled by young and beautiful empress, Senya, is a fruitful land with lush greenery. The mountains kiss the horizon, the winds whisper to the forests, the rivers flow endlessly, and the gentle warmth of Nuria's rays caresses all.

Empress Senya ruled alongside Wizard Ziva through the oversight of the water-force. The water-force, together with Ziva, constituted the lifeforce of Kingdom Svania.

Empress Senya ascended to sovereignty confident that she would win Ziva's heart. Her sole motivation was to entice Ziva into granting her permanent rule over the kingdom. So far, and much to her dismay, such undertaking had failed. Senya had achieved no more than avid graciousness from the wizard. She'd now become desperate for any opportunity at gaining permanence in her rule over Svania. With less than ninety days remining before her seven-year-reign ended, Senya's last bit of hope now hinged on the lone seer, Aries, who resided on the hill by the Pterion Springs, just outside of the forest. Many shunned Aries for her habit of using her powerful gift of foresight to trick those who sought her services.

The forest was avoided altogether for fear of the ploys of Aries. Yet, Empress Senya felt that she had no other choice but to converse with the crafty damsel. Senya slipped out of her swanky clothing and disguised herself as a commoner to pay Aries a visit. As she approached Aries' home, the door swung open, and there stood Aries.

"Aries..." Senya said, stunned by the striking beauty of the woman who now stood before her.

Aries' look was the opposite of the image Senya had imagined. The many ugly stories about Aries were a stunning contrast to her gorgeous appearance.

"Well, well, well," Aries smiled teasingly, "to what do I owe the honor of such regal visit?"

"You're beautiful," gushed Senya, eyeing Aries from head to toe. Aries' long raven hair lavishly cascaded her back, and her large brown eyes complemented her symmetric facial angles and rich mahogany hued skin.

"This must be my lucky day." Aries now stared piercingly at Senya.

"Invite me in; we have things to discuss."

"Do you not fear me?" inquired Aries.

"May I come in?" Senya asked.

"The honor is mine, dear Empress." Aries curtsied playfully and gestured for Senya to enter her lodging. Aries closed the door and motioned for Senya to be seated.

"You must be so lonely in this hideout—all of your beauty is hidden from the world."

"Dear Empress, you flatter me," Aries responded, smiling wickedly.

"But I'm compelled to ask, why are you here?" Aries locked gaze with Senya.

"I've spent the entire length of my reign trying to seduce Ziva—trying to win his heart ..."

"Ziva?" Aries interrupted, "certainly you're joking!" She shot Senya a cool smile.

"I most certainly am not," Senya shot back.

"You do know that you risk the water-force hearing us—even seeing us—for a chance to rob the kingdom of its future empresses?"

"As empress, I'm free to do whatever I wish."

"I'm sure that's why you've disguised yourself to come here," Aries quipped.

"The water-force perceives all sounds—but cannot possibly zero in on every conversation in the land. That would be ridiculous. Also, when was the last time you've heard of or witnessed punishment dispensed by the lifeforce?"

"An empress who dares to blaspheme against the very powers that made her empress in the first place."

"Don't be so melodramatic. Save your nonsense."

"I serve at your pleasure, my Empress," Aries replied in sarcasm. "Do allow me to grab blankets and refreshments—I can tell you bring me great entertainment. Aries flew across the room and was back within moments with blankets and drinks. She plopped down on a chair facing Senya sipping gleefully from her cup.

Senya was both puzzled and amazed at Aries' nonchalance. Unlike everyone else, Aries was in no way intimidated by being in the presence of the empress of the kingdom. Senya wondered how one who was so beautiful and delicate could be feared by so many.

"You may continue, dear empress," Aries said.

"My intention was to have him grant me permanent rule over the kingdom."

"I see." Aries sipped, intrigued.

"I couldn't just blatantly propose such a thing to the great wizard—and there's no other way to acquire permanence but through him."

"There most certainly isn't," Aries said distantly, "until there is."

"Until there is?" Senya echoed, her eyes suddenly alit. "You think there might be a way?"

"What specifically do you seek of me, Empress?"

"I thought I had made myself clear, Aries."

"How do you suppose I can be of any help to you?" Aries asked, sipping thoughtfully from her cup.

"I admit that I'm here seeking your help in robbing the kingdom of its future empresses—like you said."

"Hmm—and how do you suppose I would do this?" Aries gleamed.

"I'm confident that you'll think of a way."

"You know, I'm actually a bit disappointed that your plan was to coerce Ziva. You do know the wizard has no sexuality, yes?" Aries ran a gentle gaze over the goddess, then continued thoughtfully. "I'm surprised it is Wizard Ziva whom you chose to seduce, and not Wizard Qarhan of Asteria."

"Aries!" Senya said, appalled. "That's blasphemy," she scowled.

"Your intention is already blasphemous, Empress. In fact, the entire reason for your visit is most sacrilegious." Aries allowed a moment for the empress to regain composure, then she continued. "I've also recently discovered that Wizard Qarhan of Asteria has very little to no regard for Ziva. He practically considers Ziva's powers useless."

"You cannot be serious," Senya gasped. "How have you discovered this?"

"I have a deal for you." Aries smiled bountifully, ignoring Senya's question.

"Why am I not surprised?" Senya said drily. "One of your infamous tricks I suppose?"

"I mentioned nothing of tricks," Aries countered. "I said I have a deal for you," she reiterated.

"Of course," Senya replied scornfully. "But I don't recall ever asking you for a deal. I am here in the capacity of your ruler."

"I might be able to provide you with the help that you seek, but I'll need something in return."

"Let's say that you can help me—what's in it for you?"

"Convince Ziva to craft a beaming spell."

"A beaming spell?"

Aries smiled knowingly. She realized she had successfully hooked the Empress. "Ziva will need to hone his magical powers to teleport just like Wizard Qarhan. Why has no one in this kingdom ever thought to teleport—or even space warp? Have you ever asked Ziva if he's ever even considered this?"

"No—I actually have never considered it myself."

"Exactly. But why?"

"I don't know."

"Well, pose this question to Ziva. Convince him to exercise his magic muscles by trying something outside the ordinary. Think of the possibilities that could result from being transferred from one kingdom to another—instantaneously—"

"But that's it, Aries—I'm unable to think of any outcomes, let alone beneficial ones."

"Empress, he could travel unsuspectingly to other parts of the realm, and you could travel with him. Our kingdom could overrun Asteria and its rule over Nuria ..."

"Wait a minute ..."

"Why hasn't anyone ever thought of this?"

"That's not the way of our kingdom, Aries."

"Senya, having a goddess who rules forever is also not our way. Yet, that is your ambition, isn't it?"

The empress grew silent. Aries had found a way to properly muddy her ambition. She now questioned her own motives behind the need for permanent reign. She hadn't even considered whether that would mean reigning forever. Would the fountain of life remain accessible to her beyond her seven-year reign? Empress Senya had to now face the reality that enticing or tricking Ziva could not and would not work.

"Tricking Ziva won't work," she thought aloud.

"Why's that?" Aries flashed Senya a curious gaze.

"Naturally, the infamous seer would try to trick me into tricking Ziva. That's just what you do, but—it won't work, Aries. Like I've shared, I've been trying to cajole him for most of my reign but it's as if—it bounces off him. If I try to coerce him into doing what you ask, it won't work, because Ziva is not the one we need to beat. In order for me to gain what I need, I'd have to beat our lifeforce."

"Shhh!" Aries shushed. "How can you say that aloud? Do you know what it could mean for us if we're heard?" she whispered.

"I should go," Senya said, rising from her seat. "Nothing you can do for me."

"Sit back down, Empress," Aries urged softly. She allowed a moment for Senya to resume sitting. "You're so much smarter than I'd hope."

"I assume you have more for me?" Senya said.

"Ok, fine," sighed Aries. "What if I told you, that my instincts tell me, that beating the lifeforce begins with Ziva beaming from one kingdom to the next?"

"But is that even possible? If Ziva doesn't already possess this ability, could he really fashion a spell to gain it? Don't wizards either naturally possess the gift of the spell, or they remain without it?" Senya now whispered.

"But do you know this for sure?" Aries challenged.

"I—I do not—but I know the way Ziva thinks. That's the way we all think. At least I believe so."

"But have you truly considered this? I mean—if Wizard Qarhan can transport himself and others to and from kingdoms within our realm, shouldn't Ziva, who is also a wizard, be able to do the same?"

"Ziva does not possess such instincts—because it was not meant to be. We shouldn't try to corrupt that."

"Hah!" Aries spat, "says the person who seeks to rebel against the lifeforce. Empress, such hypocrisy ..."

"Watch your tongue!"

"Why not question Ziva's inability to beam across kingdoms?"

"To what benefit? He already beams within our kingdom. Many of our people have witnessed Ziva vanishing many times over the years. No reason to start questioning anything."

"But why not? Have you ever witnessed him vanishing and then reappearing in another kingdom?" Aries paused for a response but there was none. She continued as Senya noticeably wrestled with conflict. "Maybe it's time that we begin questioning things. If you convince Ziva to craft the beaming spell, then I will get you your desire."

"How?"

"How, what? How do I go about helping you—or how do you go about convincing Ziva?"

"Both."

"Find a way to convince Ziva, and I'll show you things I've foreseen." Aries replied easily.

"Have you seen the outcome of this in one of your visions, Seer?" Senya inquired.

"Just know this, your eternal reign depends upon your success with this. I mean, that's what your reign would become. Right? Eternal? Given that you and your maidens would get to drink from the fountain of life forever?"

"How do you know about the fountain of life?"

"I've seen it in my visions. Empress, do you wonder why the water-force remains so stingy with the fountain of life? Don't you think it reasonable if we all had access to it?"

"So—that's what you're after—access to the fountain of life?" Senya asked pensively.

"My intentions go beyond the fountain of life."

"Then what are they?"

"Honestly, I'm not quite sure yet. A peculiar discernment has overwhelmed me, and I strongly think it has something to do with your visit here today."

Senya was thoughtful for a moment and then asked, "Have you foreseen whether I'll succeed or fail?"

Aries downed the remaining contents of her cup, then rose from her seat. "This is where our conversation ends today. You need to leave before the water-force discerns our time together."

"What happens if I fail?"

"Absolutely nothing," Aries flashed her a wicked grin. "Your reign would simply come to an end, and another empress would take your place, as is customary."

Senya thoughtfully made her exit while pondering all that Aries had said. She wasn't at all fearful that the water-force might discern her intentions or hear of her plot with the seer, as she had always been skeptical of the water-force's omni-hearing abilities anyway.

CHAPTER THREE
Kingdom Nuria

"Svanians have opened up a portal into our corona? What nonsense is this?" Emperor Lunar scoffed.

"Sir, our Intelligence Unit informs that Wizard Ziva of the Kingdom of Svania used a spell to open up a portal that would aid him in travelling to and from our kingdom unnoticed," the aide responded.

"So then, how was he noticed?"

"Our navigation sensor detected unusual activity within our corona, Sir."

"How can we say for sure that this trespasser is Ziva?"

"Sir, the person who was stuck outside of a portal within our corona was definitely a wizard. Upon retrieving him, some of our men attempted to enter the portal, but were unsuccessful. The portal had sealed itself shut, before drying up altogether. The man we believe to be Ziva had been standing outside of the portal bellowing in an unknown tongue."

"Ziva was standing outside of the portal?"

"Yes, Sir. He was standing atop the rays of the corona."

"But that's rather impossible! How could he have been standing on top of the corona rays? Are you sure it wasn't Qarhan, Wizard of Asteria? Only he could be powerful enough to perforate time and space. Ziva has never teleported."

"Sir, we've seen the face of Qarhan, Asteria's wizard, numerous times. The person whom we have captured is not him. We are confident that it is Ziva whom we currently have in our custody."

"Well, that does seem to make sense. There are only two known wizards throughout the realm. If our captive is not Qarhan, then he must be Ziva. But what business does Ziva have with us, hopping about through portals? Has he finally grown weary of all those seductresses in Svania?"

"Sir, that remains a mystery to us. The Asterian government will be furious when we report this news to Akello, their new Chief."

"Who said anything about reporting this to Asteria? How do you suppose we would explain our discovery when we've already had to hide much of our intellect from those fools? I do not wish to hear about Asteria, nor Akello, nor any of Asteria's ill-gotten laws. Honestly, I've grown quite sick of Asterians. Who do they think they are? I'll tell you who! Asterians are ignorant bullies hiding behind a teleporting wizard. Have you ever thought about their presumptuousness? The way they have inserted themselves into the running of our kingdom? To think that we must downplay our intelligence in order to remain in their good graces! If they had an inkling of how smart we truly are, they would overthrow my rule, force us into battle, and imprison us all."

"You're absolutely right, Sir …"

"Think of all the technology, equipment and research we have had to keep hidden."

"What if we tried to educate them …?"

"Nonsense! It's impossible to convince fools that they are foolish. This would only lead to war. I vow to empower my people to outsmart the Asterian government."

"That's a vow I'm positive you'll keep…"

"Akello, Asteria's new chief, is a young, inexperienced fool with his ill-tempered father, Leo," Emperor Lunar paused his rant as Kaleb, lead intelligence officer, strode swiftly into the orbital room.

"Kaleb! What is this I'm hearing about magic being brought into our kingdom?" Emperor Lunar exclaimed.

"We have captured Wizard Ziva, Sir. He is in transit to our interrogation cell."

"Very good. Kaleb, you will go with me at once to this cell. We shall have a talk with Wizard Ziva."

"Very well, Sir. If you may walk with me to the outer gates, I have already buzzed through for a transporter to pick us up."

"Of course. Let's take a walk," Emperor Lunar replied eagerly.

"Kaleb, as lead intelligence officer, what is your take on all of this? What would motivate Wizard Ziva to open up a portal into our kingdom?"

"That is a fair question, Sir Lunar. As a matter of fact, we intend to get an answer to this question once we arrive at Ziva's cell."

The transporter announced its arrival as it approached the outer gates.

"After you, Sir Lunar." Kaleb stepped aside, making way for Lunar to step into the cab ahead of him.

They were seated and secured into the transporter which announced, *"Destination Cell 14X."*

Lunar and Kaleb stared at each other knowingly. They both understood the great opportunity they had been presented with. Although Asterians considered themselves great rulers, their greatest weapon against Kingdom Nuria was Wizard Qarhan. Until now, Qarhan had been the sole manipulator of space bending. Securing Ziva meant securing independence from the Asterians, but this also meant securing the means to travel to Planet Earth. Other alternatives would possibly take many years to execute. Yes, Ziva would be the most expedient way forward in achieving their goals.

"We won't hurt him unless we have to," Lunar uttered, breaking the silence.

"That's reasonable, given that we are not at war with the Svanians. In fact, we can attempt to strongly convince Ziva to work with us— possibly show him that an alliance with us could prove mutually beneficial." Kaleb observed as Lunar nodded in utter satisfaction.

"I agree, Kaleb. No need to hurt a Svanian. Our fight is not with them, but with the Asterians. Little do these Asterians know what Kingdom Nuria has in store for them!"

"You have arrived at your destination," the transporter announced. Emperor Lunar and Kaleb exited the transport, as guards escorted them into the cell. Upon their arrival at Cell 14X, they discovered that the small room had been vacated. Wizard Ziva had vanished.

Chapter Four
Kingdom Svania

Aries the Seer was pleased that Empress Senya had visited once more.

"Have a seat," she offered, beaming with delight and taking in Senya who stepped inside and sat— quietly wrapped up in her thoughts.

"My, my; I take it you're on board with my deal?" Aries teased as she sat to face Senya, taking in her worrisome regard.

Senya remained silent as she recollected her last conversation with Ziva. She'd cautiously planned her approach. *"Ziva," she'd begun, "have you ever considered travelling across kingdoms—the way Wizard Qarhan does?" she'd asked. The tempo of her heartbeat steadily accelerated.*

"Are you talking about beaming across kingdoms?" Ziva had seemed taken aback.

"Yes, Ziva, exactly!" Senya had said.

"Never considered it as I've always found beaming across my own kingdom fulfilling enough," Ziva had said. "Nevertheless, I do believe that I was meant to possess such a skill."

"But have you considered why not?" she'd asked.

"No," he'd replied.

"What if you should give this some thought? Could you somehow learn to recreate the spell that Qarhan uses for enchanted pathways through which he and his people travel?"

"A dimension spell!" Ziva had exclaimed.

"Anyone home?" Aries quipped, disrupting the empress' thoughts.

Senya's worrisome regard shifted to meet Aries' easy gaze.

"I convinced him," she finally spoke.

"That's very good to hear," Aries said. "Tell me more."

"Well, that's the problem, there's nothing more to tell. I haven't seen our wizard since my last conversation with him. He'd requested privacy—space—in which to explore possibilities of a dimension spell. But now he's missing."

"What do you mean, missing?"

"He's been absent--I went to his quarters to check in on him—inquire about his progress with the dimension spell...'

"Ah ha! So, it is real. Ziva is giving the dimension spell a try after all."

"I can't properly search for him and risk alerting the water-force. Where could Ziva be?" Senya asked baffled.

"Let me try a little exercise that might help us locate him. I hope you can remain calm as this process might be a bit unnerving to watch." Aries inhaled deeply, rolling her pupils to the back of her head, exposing glowing white corneas.

Senya gaped in fright—the silence deafening, and the shafts of light from Aries' eyes dizzying.

"I can see it all," Aries softly whispered, eyes aglow. "Ziva has had success with the dimension spell. But it appears that he might be in trouble ..."

"Wh- what?" Senya asked—even more terrified than before.

"Shhh! His dimension spell weakened when he arrived at Nuria. He was then discovered and captured by the Nurians."

"We have to do something ...." Senya was aghast.

"Please, do not interrupt me, Empress; you have nothing to worry about. He's managed to conjure up a spell to escape." In that instance, Aries became aware that her gift of foresight had grown more powerful as the lifeforce weakened. Aries now realized her discernment. In that moment, Aries discovered why forces beyond her comprehension had compelled her to consummate goals with Senya.

Aries had suddenly grasped that the lifeforce was unknowingly tied to the land. Therefore, Ziva's soul was tied to the land. Ziva's absence from the kingdom had ultimately weakened the kingdom's lifeforce, causing the water-force to lose its form. This shift had in turn heightened Aries' gift of foresight. Aries could now discern new powers awakening within her.

"The lifeforce has waned, but this will not last long," she said in her trance.

Senya gasped as Aries' pupils returned to their natural form. The glowing light had dissipated.

"Are you alright?" Aries asked mockingly, clearly satisfied with whatever future she had fore-seen. "I did caution this could be unnerving to watch."

"I need to go; I need to find Ziva." Senya arose flabbergasted.

"Relax, you'll soon get over the 'eye thing'. Sit back down; Ziva is already making his way back to us."

"And you've foreseen this?" Senya remained standing.

"Somewhat."

"Meaning? Is he safe or not?"

"Ziva's soul is tied to this land, but he doesn't know this. No one knows this—but me. It's no wonder we've never considered beaming across kingdoms. Not even the lifeforce is aware of this. As we speak, the power drains from the water-force—but this will not last."

"You are speaking nonsense!" Senya scowled. "You dare to taunt your goddess."

 "No, I do not. Listen to me carefully before the water-force recovers. There are four pieces to this puzzle," Aries continued. "One, Ziva's soul is tied to the land. Two, the water-force is tied to the land. Three, the fountain of youth is tied to the water-force, and four, me."

"You?" Senya asked.

"Yes, me."

"Are you trying to tell me that you wish to be a part of the lifeforce? Is that what you're after—power?"

"Wrong question. You should be asking what does it mean for us to have knowledge of the lifeforce's weakness."

"What trickery is this? You truly are evil."

"No, Empress, listen to me. You cannot share this knowledge with anyone. Regardless of your doubts about me. The water-force must not perceive any of this. Promise me."

"Or else what?" Senya scowled.

"You will ruin great marvels that have now been awakened. You must believe what you've witnessed with your own eyes. Have you so quickly forgotten my luminous eyes?"

There was momentary silence, then Aries spoke again. "The lifeforce considerably weakens during Ziva's absence from our kingdom because his soul is tied to the water-force, which is tied to this kingdom." Aries watched Senya's gaze melt into shocking realization. "Initially, I too did not know this, but felt compelled somehow, to question Ziva's beaming powers—or lack thereof. I am now a part of this as my vision has shown me that powers within me are now awakening—as a result of the lifeforce's weakness, but I have yet to perceive the reason. Certainly, the water-force would dare not integrate powers with me—and may seek to destroy me before I assimilate to my full potential."

"So, are all of our souls tied to this land?" Senya's tone was skeptical.

"No—but our essences live on in this kingdom through the power of the lifeforce"

"So, you're hoping that Ziva will use the dimension spell again?"

"This is what I meant when I inadvertently told you that your continued reign might be linked to Ziva's dimension spell."

"You wish to destroy Ziva?"

"Do you wish to reign forever?"

"How would that be possible if you destroy the lifeforce? Wouldn't we eventually die without a lifeforce in our kingdom?"

"I discern that you and all Svania's inhabitants could acquire continued life through me. You could acquire permanent reign through me. As my powers materialize—there's no telling how great I could become."

"You risked Ziva's life—the life of our people—for an experiment? You dare use me to gain power over the lifeforce? How hideous!"

A wicked smile covered Aries' face as she said, "Inform Ziva if you must, but I will defend myself against you. The water-force will know that you visited me to blaspheme against the lifeforce of this kingdom.

Accepting Aries' stunning deceit, Empress Senya made her way to the exit, dumbfounded. She intended to confess her deeds to Ziva, and reconcile with the water-force. Aries must be stopped. She would not be allowed rule over the kingdom.

"I can see the lifeforce regaining its strength." Aries also rose, following Senya. "Ziva has returned to us safely. We must not continue the conversation, to prevent the lifeforce from getting wind of our intentions. You must return to the citadel at once to welcome Ziva home."

Without responding, Senya exited the seer's cabin, barreled down the winding trail and away from the Pterion Springs where the seer lived. She adjusted her disguise and quickened her stride, refusing to be hindered by her thoughts. Moments later when she arrived at the citadel, she quickly slipped through a secret underground channel, out of her rags and back into her royal wear.

"There you are!" exclaimed her lead maiden.

"Oh, hello, there," Senya responded breathlessly, wondering if she'd been secretly discovered.

"Ziva has returned. He seems a bit tattered, but he'll survive. He's been waiting to brief you on the mission."

Thank the great force-fields. Ziva made it back unharmed. Just as Aries had predicted.

"Is everything alright, Empress? You look as though you've seen a ghost."

"Of course, I'm alright; how long have you been waiting?" Senya asked.

"Oh, not long; allow me to lead the way to Ziva. Follow me."

Senya's thoughts wandered back to the seer, fantasizing of ways in which to destroy Aries.

CHAPTER 5
SVANIA

"Sounds like quite the adventure, Wizard Ziva." Empress Senya forced a gleeful smile. She sat with her maidens huddled around a distraught looking, weakened Ziva who was barely strong enough to convey his predicament.

"It took everything I had to invoke my spell of escape," he uttered slightly shivering. "Such a close call. I still cannot fathom what could have gone wrong with my dimension spell. Honestly, it was a lot less complex to conjure than I'd expected—a few small tweaks to my existing beaming spell—and next, I was being dispensed from the portal onto Nuria's light rays."

"The portal spat you out?" the lead maiden gasped.

"It most certainly did. But ladies," Ziva cleared his throat, "I can now boldly say that I might have reached the pinnacle of my magical dexterity." He smiled weakly.

"What does this mean?" the ladies chorused.

"It means that I can beam us anywhere throughout the realm ..."

"Wait--not so fast!" Senya ruptured both Ziva's nearly breathless boastings and the women's acclamations. She sashayed over to Ziva and warmly kissed his cheek. "I think that you might be going too fast. Let's take some time to get you rested, then I'll have a talk with you at first light about your quest," Senya coerced with every intention of stalling Wizard Ziva's next attempt at a dimension spell. She needed enough time to lay it all out for the lifeforce; she was intent on confessing her actions regardless of the consequences.

"Fair enough," Ziva agreed, blissfully ignorant. "If I'm to be honest," he grunted in pain, "I actually feel a whole lot worse than I look. My muscles ache, and my body feels faint. My powers have subsided. I'll speak with you again at first light before trying to ascertain the dimension spell problem."

"You just need time to recover," Senya reassured. "Take time to rest, and we'll reconvene once you've regained your strength." Senya gestured for her maidens to join her in aiding Ziva to his quarters.

Chapter 6
Kingdom Asteria

Chief Akello anxiously paced about the counsel hall, quietly reciting his presentation. With only moments left until the council meeting, and with memories of his last conversation with his parents, he was finding his thoughts increasingly plaguing. There was no turning back now. The thought that his mother, Wanniya, had expected him to run his speech by her first, bothered him. Akello shook this thought from his head, and inwardly reassured himself. Now that he'd been coronated Chief of Asteria, he refused to be treated otherwise by anyone.

Akello brightly greeted the council members as they filtered into the council room. He took his place at the platform, maintaining an upright stance, as the council members seated themselves.

Asteria's governing body comprised twelve council members including Akello's father, Leo, as well as Qarhan, the kingdom's wizard. Akello was relieved that all of the members were present and on schedule. He was eager to get through what he considered to be his unconventional proposal. He also anticipated that the hardest part of his job as new ruler would actually be this presentation. *Asterians held steadfastly to their beliefs and traditions—blissfully ignorant.* Akello's father, Leo, seated himself next to his wife, Wanniya, at the end of the council table.
"Most esteemed council members," Akello began, "it is indeed an honor to be in your presence here today, presenting to you in the capacity of Asteria's new Chief."

"Hail, Akello!" the council members chorused.

"Please allow me to express my deepest and sincerest gratitude to all of you. I thank you for your hard work over the years in keeping Asteria on top."

"Hail, Akello!" The council members cheered in satisfaction.

"Excellent words, son!" His father beamed with pride. "I couldn't have said them better myself." Leo and the rest of the governing body shared a brief but hearty chuckle.

"The following proposals," Akello continued, eyeing his notes, "may not completely sit well on your chests." Akello was immediately aware of the sudden silence that infiltrated the room.

"Some of what I'm about to propose may shock you for one reason or another." He continued his efforts to ease his quieted audience into his presentation. His glances about the room met with inquiring stares. *Here we go. They have no choice but to hear, listen and obey.*

Akello noticed that his notepaper had dampened, so he wiped his sweaty palms into his light blue kaftan. He glimpsed his mother whispering into Leo's ear.

"My first proposal is for us to hold a special feast in honor of Leo, my father."

"Fantastic proposal!" council member six yelled.

"A fine feast it will be!" Council member eleven leaned into Leo and playfully elbowed him.

Leo smiled with pride, and whispered to his wife, "See Wanniya? Our son has this presentation covered. Nothing to worry about."

Akello nodded when his mother flashed him a gratified wink. "My second proposal is for us to build a central kitchen where our boys and girls can feed after training. Akello observed the shift in reaction. This idea meant introducing something new. The idea suggested that girls would now be included in these trainings—this was a traditional taboo.

"The next proposal," Akello continued boldly, "is to pay Kingdom Svania a visit." He looked up from his notes and continued in a matter-of-fact tone, hoping that this attitude might gain him buy-in. "Yes, honorable council, we will visit Svania to have a talk with the wizard, Ziva—convince him to lift the intrusion spell."

"Wait—is he out of his mind?" His mother looked around in shock.

Akello regarded his mother. Her outburst seemed unfitting as it was unlawful for women to speak during meetings without permission from their husband or chairperson. Suffice it to say that the council was already far too consumed with Akello's shocking proposal to even care enough to pay attention to Wanniya.

"The intrusion spell, you say?" council member number one asked before glancing over at Leo, who seemed as though he was about to combust.

"That is correct," Akello confirmed.

"The intrusion spell is what's causing us to not react to the women whenever we're in their midst," council member two clarified unnecessarily.

"I'm already keen on what the spell does, but I thank you for your insight anyway, Council member two. My intention is one of two things. I can either command that Ziva lift his spell or I can have our wizard, Qarhan, reverse it. Either way, the spell gets lifted," Akello stated definitively. By now, he'd won the war against his nerves. He listened as the council members chattered amongst themselves.

"If I may," Wizard Qarhan chimed in, "though I consider my expertise superior to Ziva's, it's quite possible that I may not be able to lift a spell that has his essence within it." Qarhan said, but quickly walked back his comment when Akello shot him an angry glance. "Nevertheless, I will certainly try," he finished off, intending to just remain silent.

"Akello," council member number one interrupted, "Ziva would never agree to lift the spell."

"But why would we need the spell lifted in the first place?" Wanniya grimaced, her voice dripping with disdain.

"To give our men versatility. Our people would be practicing inclusion and embracing diversity. This can only be a good thing," assured Akello.

"I'm sure I need not ask how you plan on practicing inclusion while embracing diversity with these women," she hissed.

"Abomination!" council member three yelled, co-signing on Wanniya's comment. "Abhorrent abomination!"

"Son, admit that this was all a ploy and proceed with the real proposal. We've wasted enough time here today already."

"Father, no, this is not a ploy—and yes, this is my actual proposal."

"The years I've wasted teaching you right from wrong. Svanian women are enchanted. It is taboo for anyone to desire them. How dare you even mention such a thing?" Leo asked, vividly overcome with bewilderment.

"My point exactly, father. We'd be able to blend cultures—study each other's ways. Father, we are the men that Svania's Kingdom needs."

"Blasphemy!" shouted council member number seven. "You are blaspheming against our gods and against the laws of our ancestors!"

"What do you mean by blasphemy? You all honor century-old laws that were put in place by mere men like us."

"I beg your pardon?" council member seven and eight questioned.

"I agree with Akello," council member five chimed in, "I think we simply owe it to ourselves to explore Akello's ideas," he implored, his tone cautious.

Wanniya and Leo exchanged scornful glances. The room is now buzzing with a cacophony of chatter.

"Esteemed Council, please allow me to complete my presentation uninterrupted. I promise to address all of your concerns once I'm through." He attempted to reconcile the dissonance.

"Give him a chance," council member eleven pleaded. "At least let him finish."

The chatter waned momentarily, and Akello resumed his pitch. "Thank you, everyone. My fourth proposal is that we invite smart and capable women to become council members—even women of Svania ..."

"Preposterous!" council member eight interjected. His outburst is ignored by Akello.

"My fifth proposal is for us to overthrow Lead Priest Lunar of Nuria— to replace him with couple of our men."

"Meaning what?" his father growled.

"Meaning a new way of life for two of our own—one from our council, the other from our military. They will act as our regents in Nuria."

"This is an utterly horrendous and absurd idea—your entire proposal is a non-starter." Leo boomed, his voice deep and steady. Akello felt a familiar throbbing in his chest—a sure sign that the dread he'd normally feel after having pushed his father to the edge, had now returned to him. With measured control, he replied, "I understand the fear of breaking our traditions."

"Breaking traditions? More like blaspheming!" council member four roared.

"Defying your chief, that's what's blasphemous," Akello replied tersely. A sudden wave of silence flooded the room. He cleared his throat and then continued, "My sixth proposal is for us to enact all of my other proposals," he concluded, with an earnest smile.

"Where is the son that I raised?" Wanniya scowled, rising from her seat. "Your father and I are so disappointed in your display here today. Leo, go ahead and cast a vote to adjourn this meeting until Akello finds his senses!"

"Mother, consider this your last council meeting," Akello advised.

Wanniya felt her heart palpitating. It's as if Akello had taken a bludgeon to her chest. "Leo, please do something," her voice breaking as she fought back tears.

"I'm so sorry, dear, I—I—our boy's faculties are clearly compromised," he stared deeply into her burning eyes.

"That's it? Leo? You're accepting our son's reductive nonsense?" The tears escaped her eyes. She stormed out the hall while Akello smiled awkwardly.

Chapter 7
Svania

Wizard Ziva was experiencing the strangest dream. In his dream, he was visited by a translucent silhouette with a feminine profile. He readily identified this being as the water-force, whose feminine contour sleekly gushed over itself, without losing its feminine construct. In this dream Ziva remained asleep, while lucidly acknowledging the presence of his sovereign half.

"We haven't met like this in centuries," he greeted, "Something must be terribly wrong."

"Your assumption is right," she replied urgently. "Ziva—you must listen to me very carefully."

"Go on," he urged, feeling uneasy.

"The lifeforce is in danger."

"Impossible."

"No, rare, but not impossible. Our powers have been compromised."

"In what way?" Ziva asked.

"Someone, somewhere is working to eliminate us."

"Eliminate us? But that's just not possible at all!"

"On the contrary, it is."

"But, how? And who would dare to be so foolish? Is it Wizard Qarhan of Asteria?"

"I doubt it."

"So, you're in doubt. If anyone is working to eliminate the lifeforce, it would have to be Qarhan. There's no one else powerful enough to even attempt such a feat."

"I've considered that possibility. But I think our perpetrator might be a lot closer to home than you think."

"But are you sure?"

"You recently worked on a dimension spell, isn't that so?"

"That is right; I'm still trying to comb through a few knots, however …"

"You concealed your actions from me," she served Ziva a penetrating stare.

Ziva's heart danced frenziedly within his chest. Hiding his deeds from the other half of himself could prove more compromising than it proved ridiculous, but he was almost home free—had his deeds not been compromised. There would be consequences, now that he'd been discovered."

"I see you've grown mute," the water-force taunted briefly, interrupting Ziva's thoughts. "You lost your power during your travel to Nuria, did you not?"

"I did, indeed."

"Well—what do you think happened when your essence was weakened?"

"I-I-didn't consider …"

"You didn't even consider this, did you?" the water-force asked, cutting him off. "Well, do allow me to enlighten you, Wizard. When you conjured your little dimension spell, your portal disintegrated because your powers were compromised, consequently collapsing your portal as well as myself."

"You collapsed?"

"Yes. But as soon as I recovered, I quickly got to work by revisiting my memories, to examine all recent chatters. Conversations between Empress Senya and Aries stood out to me. The mere thought of them both conversing with each other—privately—struck me as quite irregular, so I decided to tune in on their most recent conversations and worked my way backwards as necessary."

"How can any of this be possible?" Ziva asked, growing increasingly concerned.

"Apparently Senya's fear of stepping down as goddess has gotten the best of her. We have always been aware of her attempts at tempting you ..."

"You think her intent has been sinister?"

"I actually know for sure that they are."

"But earlier you said you weren't sure."

"Not completely—but my discernment is accurate."

"You think that our very own empress seeks to destroy us?"

"Yes, I have reasons to believe so."

"Do you hear yourself? I can't even make sense of this."

"Ziva, you must listen to me. It should come as no surprise that Empress Senya has fallen victim to Aries' cunning disposition. While you were away from the kingdom, we both lost our powers, and something happened while we were out. I just wish I could decipher what was spoken while I was incapacitated."

"So, you can't be sure these two women have turned from us?"

"I am sure of them blaspheming against us," The water-force growled. "I must warn you against continued pursuit of the dimension spell. When I revisited the chatters, I came across a conversation between Aries and Senya. Aries had managed to trick Senya into convincing you to develop a dimension spell, in exchange for information on how to rule permanently," she paused momentarily to process Ziva's bewilderment. "A permanent empress," she continued, "would have permanent access to the fountain of life, therefore never growing old, and thus, ruling our land forever. This completely deviates from the essence of the lifeforce and compromises our very existence. A permanent empress can only be made possible through destruction of the lifeforce—us."

"There has to be more to this," Ziva challenged.

"Ziva, I lost my power at the same time you lost yours. I think that my pulling you out of Nuria only accelerated depletion of my potency. So, my question now is, what is Aries' interest in your dimension spell."

"An even greater question is, why did we lose power upon my use of the dimension spell?"

"I think the seer might have foreseen this."

"Is that why you're asking me to abandon the dimension spell ..."

"I am ordering you to abandon the spell."

However, Ziva had already been too consumed to let go of this endeavor. This could be his chance to surpass Wizard Qarhan of Asteria.

"In addition," the water-force continued, "I need you to proceed with a spell to remove Aries' vision."

"Wait a minute- you're asking me to abandon the spell and blind Aries?"

"Only temporarily until we gain control of the situation. Our kingdom depends on it."

"What if your suspicion is wrong? What if its Wizard Qarhan that's responsible for all of this?" Wizard Ziva asked.

"After all I have shared, you remain reluctant? We do not have much time left—you're about to awake from your sleep. You must hurry! Perform the spell now, while you're still asleep. When you awake, abandon the spell and bring Empress Senya to me. Aries will not be able to foresee our plot, as long as you execute the spell of blindness in your dreams."

"Hence your interruption of my sleep."

"Indeed. Aries must have no knowledge of this. I came to you while you slept to avoid the Seer's gift of foresight. You must trust me on this. Should you go against me once more, it might be the end of us."

"Please reconsider, as our powers are now being restored. Let me help you solve this mystery in a gentler manner ..."

"Gentler manner? Ziva, for an immortal being, you speak and act so foolishly. Our powers should never have been meddled with in the first place. Should this event repeat itself, we may never survive it. Once Aries' vision is removed, her gift of foresight will be removed along with it, allowing us room for resolution. Aries is asleep as we speak—and she dreams. You must also summon the being of hindrance, to trail her once she goes blind. Do it now while she dreams, Ziva!"

Chapter 8
Kingdom Svania

Aries, the Seer, had drifted off to sleep with a million thoughts racing through her mind. Would Empress Senya successfully convince the wizard to conjure a dimension spell? Despite the seer's discernment that another dimension spell would annihilate the lifeforce, hard as she tried, Aries could not foresee a future in which she ruled the kingdom. This had struck her as stunningly odd. Why had she felt so blinded? Right before she fell asleep, she'd revisited her most recent vision of her most immediate future—a future beyond which she'd been unable to foretell. She'd foreseen herself getting acquainted with, and becoming smitten by, a most attractive-looking young man. The vision had baffled her because Wizard Ziva's intrusion spell protected against such occurrences. Falling in love with outsiders was unheard of. Unless the intrusion spell would somehow be broken—a sign that the lifeforce was terminated—yet Aries knew she was clutching at straws, as her gift of seeing beyond the near future eluded her.

Another terrifying concern for Aries was also her inability to fathom the face of her alluring prospect.
It was a wonder that Aries had finally managed to doze off. Wizard Ziva suddenly appeared to her—in her dreams, beckoning at her—as if he had a message to convey. Curious, she inclined her ears, but then quickly realized she'd been mistaken. Ziva wasn't trying to convey a message at all. He was simply muttering a chant.
"Virtue of the realm,
Forces of derision,

Remove from your helm,
The Seer's gift of vision."
"Ziva, what are you doing?" she yelled. But Ziva continued his chant.
"You must stop this nonsense! Ziva, stop this now!"
Aries watched as Ziva raised both his arms in fervency, then returned them to a clasp.
"It has been done," he murmured before vanishing.
Aries leaped from her sleep and off the bed. The place was dark, so she breathlessly reached for the uplighter, but she couldn't find it as the place was too dark. Her heart pounded mercilessly against her chest as her nightmare ignited. What had Wizard Ziva done?

Ziva awakened from his dream with a thunderous headache. His throat ached from dryness, and his heartbeat intensified. He palmed his forehead with one hand while using the other to raise himself out of bed. Light rays from the early dawn seeped gently through the cracks of his den and into the corner of his eyes, making his headache even more excruciating. He retrieved his water jug and downed all its contents. *The aftermath of casting a spell while asleep.* Such a feat had further ravaged his already spent powers. Ziva hobbled into his workroom to retrieve and drink his special pterion vitae elixir, a concoction of jhinge tree sap and hazel flower juice. The potion was used to take the edge off dream-spell hangovers, so Ziva sat and waited for its effects to activate. He'd been tempted in the past to discard the potion, given its lack of use. Fortunately, he'd held on to it, and an excellent decision that had turned out to be.

Ziva leaned back against his workbench, taking deep breaths while dismissing thoughts of Aries the Seer, and the impairment he'd caused her. Overwhelmed, he considered options for beseeching the water-force—he needed to get her to see reason. There must be a way to convince the water-force to release Senya and Aries from punishments. Instead, the focus should be geared towards the Asterian government. Surely, Wizard Qarhan was far more answerable to such gross misuse of powers. If anyone was to blame, it should be Qarhan. But such efforts would have to be paused to allow Ziva time to quickly refine his dimension spell, while averting any detection by the water-force.

Moments later, Ziva was back at it again. Though still weak, he was re-energized as effects of the elixir kicked in. There could be no lingering or waste of time. If he was able to quickly polish the dimension spell, then he would have a more substantial case in favor of Senya and Aries. Ziva was convinced that fixing the dimension spell would save both women, as well as the institution of the kingdom.

He discarded the remains of the voyage elixir he'd used for the previous dimension spell and concocted a new potion. This time, he added silversalt in efforts of heightening the focus of the new portal's endpoint to ensure accuracy in landing. He closed his eyes and inhaled deeply, still aching from every movement. Nevertheless, he was determined to see this mission through completion. The only way to ensure precision was to try out the new and improved dimension spell—once again—by himself. Ziva, in his fatigued state, set his destination for Kingdom Octushi, the desolate and bare kingdom. He reasoned that this time, should his spell once again

malfunction, then his exploits would remain undetected, as there was nobody in Octushi to detect them. Ziva poured the potion onto the floor in a circular motion around him, then chanted:
"Spirit of Svania, forces of Zannus,
Sharpen my strength, heighten my focus,
Guiles of my lineage, descend upon me,
Bring me straightway to the kingdom of Octushi."

A portal appeared and opened in front of Ziva, right in the middle of his workroom. He stepped inside and was immediately whisked away as the portal folded into itself before vanishing. Ziva's voyage to Octushi was a brief but turbulent one. Moments later he was flung from the portal and sent crashing into the dusty wilderness of Octushi. Once again, he was immediately overcome by a familiar feeling of weakness and anxiety—the same feelings he'd experienced as his powers failed him in Nuria. How could this be? Highly cognizant of his self-inflicted dilemma, Ziva quickly chanted a return spell, but did so to no avail. His powers had become inoperable, and unlike before, he was completely cut off from the water-force. Ziva knew right away that he was dying. Too weak for regrets, he closed his eyes and allowed himself to fade away.

Chapter 9
Kingdom Asteria

Akello sprang from his nightmare and leaped to the floor. Beads of sweat dripped from his brow as he recollected the terrible dream in which he defied his father and disappointed his mother. He felt his heart splinter as reality hit him. This was not a nightmare, but a collection of memories from the council meeting of his induction earlier that day. He had presented several proposals that were considered unfavorable by the council men. Akello sighed deeply and sprawled out on the floor, looking up at the ceiling. Handling his parents—his mother, in the way he'd done, left a bad taste in the back of his throat. He explored his thoughts for possible gentler alternatives but found none. He'd always anticipated the arrival of this day, a day when he could freely share his vision for the kingdom with his people. He'd considered the prospect of rejection, yet the reality of it had been far more brutal.

Akello planned on calling a meeting with council men one, two, five, six and eleven. Later he would meet with the remaining council to discuss this earlier meeting. He sighed at this thought because he knew that this could possibly lead to more outrage amongst the men who remained loyal to his father. Akello hoped that his upcoming meetings would progress a whole lot smoother than that of his induction. Too many years had been wasted honoring laws that were centuries old. Akello's thoughts wandered to Nuria—a kingdom of intelligent and forward-thinking people. How could his father or anyone else not see that the Nurians' superior intellect puts their kingdom at a disadvantage? Akello's thoughts wandered to Qarhan's spiel about being unsure of his abilities to break Ziva's spell. He then revisited thoughts of the Nurians. He wondered who would best fit the role of Asteria's ambassador. Overthrowing Lord Lunar had been long overdue and Akello hoped that it wasn't too late to do so.

"Are you suggesting that we invade their kingdom?" councilman one asked. He stared intently into piercing eyes that stared back at him. "How can we even be sure that Ziva will break his intrusion spell?" asked councilman six.

"Can we be certain that our wizard, Qarhan, is able to break Ziva's intrusion spell?" asked councilman two.

"Well, it wouldn't hurt for Qarhan to start trying," councilman five replied. "As for Kingdom Octushi, it's nothing more than a cursed kingdom with no signs of life."

"The only way we can ensure continuity in our rule is to take in and study Svanian women, and replace Nurian leader, Lunar, with one of our own men. We will reprioritize my goals in such order," replied Akello.

"So, you have not reconsidered any of it—not even the goal of having Ziva's intrusion spell lifted?" councilman six asked.

"Council, what do you really think? Please—be honest with me. Forget about the nonconformity of my goals; just tell me what you truly think about them. I chose you to be a part of this meeting because I have recognized your openness to my proposal."

The men silently contemplated Akello's question. Akello is pleased at how smoothly this second meeting was progressing in the absence of the remaining councilmen.

"Controversy set aside," councilman eleven began, "I consider your proposals quite adventurous. I mean—I have been close friends with your father for many years now—but your pitch has got me thinking. No one would dare put forward the items you have presented to us."

"I agree," admitted councilman six. "I've just been too ashamed to say it out loud. The idea of connecting with Svanian women appeals to me," he shrugged while looking around the room for support.

"I agree," said councilman two. "I think it's foolish to deny the vast intellect of Lord Lunar and his people. The Nurians could very well destroy our kingdom with weapons unknown to us. We can't be sure what to expect from the Nurians, so we must keep a watchful eye on them."

"Those are true words," councilman six chimed in. "We must not fear seeking answers and must study the Svanian women. We must question existing laws and seek wisdom, so that we may become advanced, as the Nurians are advanced."

"We could consider enslaving them," said councilman five.

"I have listened to each of you and I'm happy that you are all on board with the ideas. This meeting has been quite productive, and I will consider all your suggestions, as you have considered mine. We will work together as a team to advance ourselves into a new age ..."

"Of what new age do you speak?" his father yelled, storming into the room alongside the remaining four councilmen who had not been invited to Akello's pre-meeting discussion.

"Akello, you dared to conduct a meeting without me—without the entire council including Wizard Qarhan?" Leo scowled.

"Father, I am glad that you are here ...."

"I find that very interesting given that neither I nor my colleagues were invited to this meeting," Leo said, cutting Akello off. "And where is our Wizard?"

"I planned on inviting you to a separate and more formal meeting, which may commence at this very moment if you wish—given that we are all now present ..."

"Such blatant disregard for the laws of our kingdom. Who authorized you to conduct meetings in this way?"

"Father, you and your comrades are welcome to be seated so that we may continue the discussion." Akello motioned for the others to leave the room.

"Pardon me, but if your intent is to continue your secret discussion, why are the rest of us leaving?" councilmen seven and eight chorused. Upon hearing this comment, councilmen six and eleven stopped, while five, two and one continued their swift exit.

"Sharp observation indeed, comrades," Leo fumed.

"Father, you fixate on the wrong things ..."

"How dare you spit upon our intellect!" yelled councilmen three and four.

"Please have a seat ..."

"Be quiet, boy! We refuse to sit with you, let alone listen to any further nonsense!" yelled yet another.

"Watch your tongue, gentlemen. I am your chief after all," Akello replied coolly.

"Chief? What chief? You're a far cry from being our ruler," hissed councilman three.

Akello listened quietly as an angry chatter erupted amongst the men. He lost track of whom was yelling what. It is his father's penetrating silence that wounded him the most, but Akello found the strength to push past that familiar feeling of dread to address the men once more. "Father—gentlemen," he said calmly, "I understand your frustration with me. You feel that I have let you down." He paused briefly to regard each of the men, a few of them awkwardly shifted about. His father was shaking his head in revulsion.

"We cannot grow as a people if we cannot accept change. We cannot continue to do the same thing forever—this would be madness. Our people should seek more knowledge. Surely there's much more to learn from the Svanians—for instance, why shouldn't the wizards of both kingdoms collaborate? Why shouldn't we learn more about Svanians? So many of my female colleagues long for the chance to join our battalion—even our council. All women should be presented with that option—even Svanian women."

"Son, this can never happen. It's just not the Asterian way."

"But it's about to be, father. That's the message I've been trying to convey. I want to open our doors to a new age ...."

"We're not buying the taboo you're selling," shouted councilman three.

"My intention was not to offend you, but to conduct a meeting where all attendees can freely air their opinion without being judged. Your reluctance is why I hadn't included you in my earlier discussion ..."

"Wait a minute," his father interrupted, "are you trying to tell us that the councilmen who just walked out of here are on board with your leud proposition?"

"We are on board with our new chief," councilman eleven chimed in, while councilman six nodded in agreement. Akello was inwardly gleeful that both six and eleven had stayed behind to defend him, instead of leaving with the others.

"I will not allow it ..."

"Father, you have no other choice."

"Son—I am not the father you want to make an enemy out of."

"Father, I am not the son who will hesitate to relocate you to Kingdom Nuria if I have to."

"How dare you?" his father growled. His piercing gaze alerted Akello that Akello has successfully driven the final nail into their father-son-relationship coffin. For all Akello knew—all hope for preserving the remnants of his bond with his mother had also been irreparably severed.

"You, filth!" councilman two yelled.

"That is not the proper way to address your new chief!" Wizard Qarhan scowled as he entered the room. All heads turned in his direction.

"I hereby release you from this council," Qarhan declared.

"I beg your pardon?" councilman two challenged.

"Should you attend another one of our meetings, I'll have you imprisoned." Akello chimed in, inwardly thankful for Wizard Qarhan's arrival. Akello made a mental note to always have the wizard present at all future meetings.

The men still did not budge, but instead, remained standing with their jaws in their hands.

"Wizard, please show these men that we aren't playing games." Akello commanded.

Immediately Wizard Qarhan conjured a ball of lightning within an outstretched palm. He motioned to strike when the rebellious councilman suddenly fled the room in fright. Wizard Qarhan lowered his palm and the ball of light vanished, and the room quieted. Akello felt his lips parting slightly giving way to a triumphant smile. "For the rest of you," he said, adeptly averting his father's deadly glare, "I look forward to your compliance with my authority. Thank you, and you are all dismissed for today."

Akello, Wizard Qarhan and councilmen six and eleven watched pensively as the other stormed out of the room. Akello felt the urge for a distraction. What better distraction than an immediate visit to the kingdom of the temptresses? He would need to summon his guards, and councilmen one, two and five right away.

Akello did not see the tear that escaped the corner of Leo's eyes as he left the room. In fact, none of the other men did.

Chapter 10
Kingdom Nuria

Upon his discovery that Wizard Ziva had vacated his cell, Lunar dismissed Kaleb and returned to his garret in disappointment. He'd been quite hopeful about collaborating with the wizard, but any such hope had now vanished with Ziva. Numerous thoughts crossed his mind. Lunar wondered about the wizard's motive for attempting to visit Nuria undetected. It was fortunate that their navigation-rooter had uncovered Ziva's presence in the corona, but also unfortunate that Ziva had escaped with some knowledge of Nuria's true technological advancement. No telling of what he'd seen especially when Kaleb's team used technology to retrieve him from the air into which he'd been flung by the portal. It was highly likely that Ziva might reveal confidential details to the Asterians, which could result in the ultimate battle for freedom. Warfare was now a possibility worth examining. If war was on the horizon, then Lunar's people would need to face it head on. Re-directing focus to combat logistics would have to be prioritized, as the Nurians are finding it increasing difficult and backwards to hide their ingenuity.

Lunar considered the decrees that tied his people to Asterian rule. He was angered by the seemingly dated traditions that hindered the freedom of his people. He'd grown weary of questioning his own adherence to subservient norms that might eventually stagnate his kingdom. The rule had always been to acquiesce to the Asterians because they possess a wizard, and the Nurians do not. But the time had come to rise up. It was near impossible to fight magic using intellect, but Lunar could feel an impending insurgence deep inside his bones. Lunar and his team had constructed a vast collection of technological equipment, materials and weapons—and it is time to put these innovations to the test. They had been successful so far, in out-maneuvering the Asterians by keeping things simple, and concealing their technology. But how long would it be before Wizard Qarhan saw right through them. Lunar shook his head at this thought. How had it never occurred to Wizard Qarhan to use his magic to spy on them? Why had it also not occurred to Wizard Ziva to do the same. To think that they can conjure portals out of thin air, but find it impossible to even foresee things?

"Why has no one ever thought of this? How has this only just now occurred to me?" Lunar contemplated deeply. If this thought was now occurring to him, then it would only a matter of time before it occurred to someone else—the enemy—because that was how he viewed Asteria—as his enemy. Not to mention the kingdom's new, young chief, Akello. No telling what new plans this new, young chief had up his sleeves. A young chief would be too eager to flex his influential muscle. Also, there was another factor to consider—Wizard Qarhan. If Lunar were to be honest with himself, he must admit that he desperately feared Wizard Qarhan, as none of his science can ever compete with Qarhan's magic. Lunar's thoughts then shifted to Kaleb's goal of relocating the Nurians to Planet Earth.

"Would you like some berries, dear?" Lunar's wife popped her head inside his study. Lunar jolted from his thoughts. "What's bothering you dear? You don't look so good," her tone receptive.

"Huh, just matters of the land," Lunar responded with a sigh "Berries will be fine—also some tea, please."

"Sure," she said smiling pleasantly, "but only if you accompany me to the tearoom."

"Very well." Lunar rose from his chair and headed towards the tearoom with his wife.

"Talk to me. Tell me what's on your mind," his wife implored. So, Lunar began.

His wife listened keenly to his account of Ziva's bizarre visit, capture and escape. Lunar thoroughly explained how the event had stirred his thoughts, urging a new viewpoint of insurgence.

"It only makes sense," Lunar argued, "because we are the intelligence headquarters of the realm."

"My dear, I do agree with you that as the most intellectually forward kingdom, we should be the ones to rule the realm. However, war is just not our way. We could never live with ourselves for mirroring the Asterians."

"We wouldn't be mirroring them. We would be reclaiming our dignity."

"I understand that you are feeling frustrated …"

"No, not frustrated, subdued. I am feeling subdued. No more; we must fight back."

"But what about their wizard?" she asked pointedly.

"Which always brings us back to square one," Lunar opined.

"You know what I don't understand?" she said.

"What's that?" Lunar asked.

"How is it that for all these years, Qarhan had been able to skip dimensions to other kingdoms, but had never been able to use his magic to catch us?"

"You are a woman after my own heart," Lunar admitted with a smile. "I've been asking myself those very questions."

"If I share with you my recommendation for solving this problem, promise me you will use it."

"I- wh- what recommendation could you possibly have to give this time?" he quizzed.

"Promise me, Lunar."

"Very well, I promise."

"Set aside any intimation of war."

"But—my love …"

"Just a moment. Revisit the true purpose of our existence. Let us use our wisdom to find the means for instant-travel, not just to earth, but also any other kingdom we desire."

"I'm listening."

"Your navigation rooter picked up distress signals from Ziva's portal, correct?"

"Correct," Lunar confirmed.

"What if remnants of the portal could be recovered and studied?"

"We could possibly re-erect Ziva's portal … or even erect one of our own!" Ziva gasped. He flashed his wife a wicked grin. "Thank you, my love."

"Just remember, I am the intelligence headquarters of our marriage," she beamed.

"Indeed, you are." Lunar kissed her passionately. He was relieved to have discovered a possibly feasible solution after all.

Chapter 11
Kingdom Svania

Empress Senya took a few sips from the fountain of life then strolled outside of the citadel into her private garden—well—it would be her garden until her reign ended. She sat on a large, smooth rock overlooking the shallow pond sited at the heart of the garden. The stillness of the pond's pure surface glistened at each touch of Nuria's light rays. Until now, this spot had been her favorite hideaway; however, nothing seemed pleasing anymore. Her life had taken a turn for the worst. Understanding there was no way out of her predicament but through it, Senya mentally braced herself for her forthcoming conversation with Wizard Ziva. She inhaled deeply and took in the gentle warmth of her surroundings, acutely regretting having solicited Aries' help at all. How could she have sought collaboration with Aries? She had been chosen by the lifeforce to rule for seven years, and this was her seventh year of being empress of the land. Though her time as empress was nearly through, this had not been the complicated, life-threatening ending she had anticipated. Certainly, she would have been much better off throwing a great feast and merriment—she could have simply just settled for going out in style before yielding to her successor—whomever that would be. But it was now too late for such plans.

Empress Senya briefly pondered the seer's mention of ruling forever. Until that moment she hadn't realized that the longer she ruled, the longer she could possibly maintain her access to the fountain of life, which meant eternal dominion over the kingdom of Svania—a bold and clever idea that none of her predecessors had even dared to consider. How could she then be faulted for such a desire? Yet, the price to pay is far too high, almost impossible to fulfill. She dared not sell her soul. Senya quietly scoffed at herself for pushing her maidens away whenever they approached her with ideas for an exit-party. How cruel, because the end of her reign would also affect her maidens. It was undoubtedly a bad idea not to have been more inclusive with them in the first place. Yet the thought of returning to common living seemed so entirely dreadful, and this is the thought that had led Senya to this horrible moment. It even seemed as though this moment was just as awful as not being able to reign for longer, but Senya was ready to right her wrongs, regardless of the dreadfulness of it all. She just hoped that it wasn't too late.

Senya knew she had to do something soon, although many questions and concerns plagued her. For instance, where did the seer acquire power to light up her eyes during the trance? How had Aries been able to see Ziva's capture? How is it possible for Aries to see beyond Kingdom Svania? If so, could it really be that her gift is strengthened when the lifeforce is weakened? Had this been her goal for ultimately trying to destroy the lifeforce? There were many questions that needed answers, yet the one thought that seemed most critical—despite Senya's active dismissal of it—is this: *who was Aries, really?*

Empress Senya knew it was imperative that she spoke to Ziva immediately, but not before visiting with the seer one last time. She quickly scanned her surroundings, adjusted her hooded disguise, and knocked on Aries' door. She was surprised that the seer hadn't discerned her visit. Senya allowed a moment to pass before knocking again. Still no answer. *Perhaps she was away.*

She decided to make herself comfortable by the hedges next to the seer's lodge, but just as she was about to sit, she heard the cherolith growl. The door slowly opened and Aries cautiously stepped outside, guided by her six-footed pet. Senya gasped with fright at the sight of the creature, but her curiosity was heightened even more when Aries wildly affixed her stare to something other than Senya's eyes.

"What are you looking at?" Senya asked curiously.

"I'm glad you came back," she yelped.

"Why do you stare over my shoulders? Afraid to look me in the eyes?" Senya asked, turning her head briefly to scan for the object of the seer's gaze. When Aries exploded in tears, Senya was taken aback. Nevertheless, she snarled, "another one of your tricks?"

Aries' dried her face with the back of her free hand while busily calming the cherolith with the other. "Easy girl," she whispered through even more tears.

"Huh! That thing is female?"

"You shouldn't have come here, Empress," Aries wept gently.

"It's not as if I'm very excited to be here," Senya's glare now restrained by Aries' tears.

"Just watch what you say ..."

"I have questions. Do you hear me, Aries the seer?" Senya yelled interrupting Aries. "I am your empress, and you must give me what I ask."

"Ziva has blinded me," Aries replied quickly.

Senya gasped in horror. The cherolith continued to growl.

"Aries, another trick up your sleeve?" Senya asked curiously. But Aries was unable to control her tears. Senya allowed her a moment to cry. Moments later, with blood-shot eyes, Aries finally composed herself and proceeded to sit on the ground.

"Sit, girl, I'm ok," she said to the cherolith who immediately sat next to her.

When she gazed up and her stare once again missed Senya's searching eyes, Senya was struck by the sudden realization that Aries must have truly gone blind.

"Aries, tell me what's going on," she gasped.

"I've been stripped of my gift—my sight is gone—and so are my visions," Aries mourned once more.

"How can this be?" Senya asked feeling utterly unsettled.

"I already told you how," Aries answered sniffling.

"I'm confused ..."

"He appeared to me in a dream—through which he casted a spell to remove my gift," Aries explained.

"You're not making any sense—I'm confused—who appeared to you?"

"I never would have even considered that such a thing was at all possible," Aries explained.

"Such a thing such as what?"

"While I slept, Ziva appeared to me—in my dream. At first, I thought he had a message for me—I thought he was trying to caution me about something. But then I realized what was really happening." Aries paused briefly, shaking her head in disbelief of the memory. Wiping away tears she continued. "In my dream, Ziva chanted a spell to have my sight removed and my gift severed with it. I then arose from my sleep unable to see or foresee."

"But—that's not possible. When I last saw Ziva he was far too weak to even speak, let alone blind you through your dreams. I'm sure that you are mistaken."

"Before losing my sight—and my gift—I realized that they go hand in hand—anyway, I'd spent days battling to see the future—but all I could see was myself falling in love with a faceless man—somewhere in the near future. I'd been so puzzled about this, but now I finally understand. I think that when I meet this man—I won't be able to see him—which is why…"

While Aries rambled on, Senya's thoughts drowned her out. Senya looked towards the woods in the direction of the Pterion Springs where the water-force abided. Has the seer gone mad? The beautiful and spirited temptress that Senya had visited only a short while ago was gone. In her place stood a pitiful, weeping wretch pretending to be blind.

"What does any of this even means?" Senya questioned.

"Ziva has put a spell on me. He did this while I was dreaming. This is why I was unable to foresee losing my vision and gift. Every ounce of my gift has vanished."

"So—you're saying that Ziva executed a spell while both of you dreamt, because if —if he had performed the spell awake—you could have foreseen it?"

"Yes! That's it!" Aries said with relief.

"Why would Ziva do this?" Aries asked, then paused with realization. Aries could be lying, but if she was not, if she told the truth, then Ziva knew! The lifeforce knew their plan. If this is the case, then she was out of time. She would much prefer a life as a commoner over a life without her sight. If the water-force knew and has done this thing to Aries, then she would be next.

"I have to go," Senya concluded.

"So, you understand," Aries remarked knowingly, while slightly sniffling away remnants of tears.

"If you speak the truth, then all of this is your fault."

"Please, Empress, plead with Ziva for me," Aries implored. But Senya had already dashed off.

As she hurried home, Senya recalled granting Ziva time alone to recoup. She wondered whether Ziva had been spending his time betraying her instead. Senya shrugged at this ridiculous thought, as the cause of this detriment was due to her own betrayal. She had inadvertently colluded with Aries against the lifeforce, and there's just no excuse for that. Senya sailed through the gates of the Citadel and barreled towards Ziva's den.

"Ziva, it's me, Empress Senya. Please let me in!" she breathlessly pleaded while pounding on Ziva's door. She paused a moment for a response, but there was none. Something eerie was amidst.

"Ziva!" she bellowed, trying to catch her breath. No response.

Senya sank to the floor resting her back against the door. Inhaling deeply, she tilted her head backwards and closed her eyes. The door gently gave way as it slid open, causing Senya to catch herself before toppling backwards into the den.

"The door is open?" she asked herself aloud. "Ziva, I thought you had casted a protection spell over your den," she said as she nervously entered the room.

"Ziva, please grant me one moment to explain everything. Where are you?" She asked, cautiously wandering about Ziva's lodging. She felt her insides ripping open as Ziva's non-responsiveness intensified her fears.

Chapter 12
Kingdom Asteria

Akello had spent much time re-prioritizing his proposal, reorganizing the governmental body of Asteria, as well as rounding up the right men for his forthcoming trips.

His first trip, a visit to Svania to meet with Ziva as well as the many women in the kingdom was first and was due to occur at any moment. His second trip, a visit to Kingdom Nuria, was tentatively slated based on the success of his Svania trip. His third trip to Octushi was pending the success of the trips to Svania and Nuria. He intended to finalize his plans for both kingdoms before tackling the uncertainty of Kingdom Octushi, the land of bareness.

"It's a glorious day for travelling," beamed councilman eleven.

"Even more glorious to be travelling with you, Eleven." Akello retorted cheerfully.

"The honor is mine, young sir," Eleven said.

"Indeed," Akello replied feeling joyful at the prospect of his goals coming to fruition. He was at peace with his decision to restructure the council and was glad to have ridded the governmental body of disruptive, dangerous men.

"Eleven, let's take a walk," he said.

"Indeed," Eleven replied, making his way with Akello to the Port of Origin. This Port was the common location from which Asterian wizard, Qarhan, often launched his portal for departure with the group to the various kingdoms of the realm.

"Congratulations, leader!" a few passers-by cheered.

"Thank you!" Akello replied eagerly. Further along the path a group of young women blushed and giggled as Akello and Eleven walked by. Akello nodded in acknowledgement. Eleven chuckled.

"Tell me, Eleven, in all honesty, do you believe I've begun my rule heavy handedly?" Akello asked.

"Well," Eleven began, "you are very popular—obviously. You are loved by your people," he chuckled again. "I think you're getting a very good response overall."

"Yes—but women have always responded positively to me. I can't say that this accounts for Asterians as a whole," Akello countered.

"Your people love you, Akello."

"Then why am I estranged from even my own parents?"

"You must understand that your parents are devastated by your choices," Eleven said matter-of-factly.

"Thanks for the reassurance," Akello said sullenly.

"No, allow me to finish. Akello, you are very brave to have embraced the challenge of stepping into a new age. You have defied your parents so your own vision for a new age can live—so that your people can live. Tradition may not be the only way to go. We need to become inspired and innovative. You are the face of that. And we, your people, believe in you."

"You're sure?" Akello's eyes lit up once more.

"Positive," Eleven said smiling. "As close as I was to your father, I have to admit your perspective is quite stimulating."

"Or are you just stimulated by the idea of us traveling to Svania?" Akello quipped.

"Nonsense!" Eleven chuckled. "And don't believe that you're the only one your father has renounced."

"I'm well aware that he's upset with you for standing by me."

"Precisely. But, I, like you, have to stand up for what I believe in. I refuse to base my decision to serve my kingdom, solely on your father's validation."

"I get it—but what about my mother?"

"Your mother loves you more than life itself. She'll come around some day. But right now, you must remain focused on achieving your goals. Prove to your parents that you are a great leader," Eleven returned Akello's smile and together they entered the Port of Origin.

"Good to see you, Chief," the men greeted Akello, "Council member Eleven, welcome."

"Likewise," Akello and Eleven replied in unison.

"Where is our wizard?" Akello asked, scanning the area for Qarhan.

"Wizard Qarhan present," yelled Qarhan, making his way through the gathering with councilmen one, two, five and six.

"Very well, let us begin our journey," Akello commanded. "Wizard Qarhan, launch the portal! We are headed for Kingdom Svania to see Wizard Ziva!"

Chapter 13
Kingdom Svania

Aries, the now impaired seer, had been working tirelessly at gaining self-sufficiency, quickly. Despite her dilemma, she was determined to gain independence. Surely, if she'd foreseen her blindness, there might have been something she could have done to prevent it. At the very least, she could have started her self-reliance practice a lot sooner, or even—not falling asleep that fateful night—or at all, thus preventing Ziva from carrying out his spell, or foiling any of his plans by getting rid of him herself. She could have done something. But the lifeforce had outsmarted her, which showed that when one thinks of herself as the cunningest, there is always someone far more cunning.

Aries' thoughts shifted to Senya. She wondered how the empress was faring, and whether she had made any progress convincing Ziva to forgive them both. Aries no longer felt like sitting about feeling helpless and hopeless. She needed to pay a visit to the wizard and plead to him herself. She settled on a plan for making her way to the Citadel to find Wizard Ziva on her own. She would use her cherolith as her guide in travelling out and about in the open, by way of the local market so that on her way to the citadel, she may employ the services of a personal handmaiden. Her pantry was also in need of restocking—so coming out of hiding was now a must. Aries gathered the necessities for her journey, omitted her usual disguise, and headed through the door alongside her pet cherolith. She was off to see Ziva, the wizard of Svania.

Chapter 14
Kingdom Nuria:
Reverse Engineering of the Portal

Lord Lunar's suggestion to use a scientific approach to reverse engineer Ziva's magical portal was deemed ingenious by intelligence officers. Immediately, the team joined collaborative efforts with Nuria's lead physicists and engineers to achieve the monumental task of producing a portal. A particulate booster was used to capture and preserve remnants of background microwave particles from Ziva's portal. The mission was labeled as classified and given top-most priority in the land. For centuries, Nurians have been secretly examining Asteria's ability to travel faster than light—sans the magical aspect, of course. They assembled theories around the possibility of spacetime warping—now finally, there was an actual opportunity to speed up the research process to attain the answers they so desperately sought. Lunar and his team worked diligently to investigate the properties of the various particles retrieved, particularly the exotic ones. The crew rarely stopped for a break—they had even become sleep deprived. Alas, however, a great discovery was made.

"Got it!" shouted Taurus, "today, thanks to Ziva's portal, we can officially say that we have successfully gained massive perspective on decades of research."

"What is it?" questioned the others excitedly.

"Come and take a look at this, it will leave you breathless," Taurus boasted.

Everyone eagerly gathered around Taurus.

"Lunar, please be my first guest. Have a look through these lenses."

"Ok," Lunar complied, "what am I looking at?" he asked while peering through the lenses.

"I was able to construct a microscopic rotating blackhole. Look at how the starfield in front of it is being dragged and distorted by the gravitational forces."

"Magnificent!" Lunar gasped in awe.

"One of our main theories can now be addressed—principally the curvature of spacetime and its direct relation to the energy and momentum of matter and radiation."

They all directed celebratory cheers at Taurus, who was beside himself. Lunar was pleased at the tremendous progress they had made. The hardest part of the research seemed to have come to an end. Finally, they could take a moment to replace their anxiety with triumph.

"I hate to be the bearer of bad news, but I too made a similar discovery, but had to set it aside pending conclusion of my current study," said Darius, lead physicist. Immediately the room hushed.

"What do you mean?" Taurus asked.

"Well, the behavior of some of these particles defy our known laws of physics," he replied.

"Do explain," requested Lunar.

"Given that we've never encountered such particles, we cannot, at this time say for sure that Taurus is right, and that his discovery fully addresses relativity. Look—some of these particles have a negative mass, which is why I didn't ..."

"Precisely!" Taurus said, cutting off Darius. "Some of the particles have a negative mass. But I have managed to use such negative mass to stabilize the blackhole properties of the portal!" Taurus radiated with pride.

"Thus, creating a wormhole—so communication is never lost during passage," Darius gasped.

"Exactly," Taurus confirmed.

"Genius," replied Darius, "then given this stabilization effect, the point of horizon vanishes, causing a safe path for the traveler from one dimension to the next!"

"Brilliant indeed," Darius nodded in agreement, "You have outsmarted me."

The gathering cheered and shouted with joy.

"So, the idea now," Caleb stated when everyone had quieted, "is to maximize the quantum effects of the microscopic wormhole to construct a macro-wormhole that warps spacetime, connecting one place to another."

"Yes," beamed another physicist, "we will start by ensuring that whatever goes into this wormhole portal, comes back out."

"Terrific! Let us first experiment with Caleb—throw him into the portal and see what happens." Everyone engaged in a bout of laughter.

"Alright everyone, there's still more work left to be done." Lunar smiled.

"We must continue to work quickly to finalize our goal before the Asterians' next visit."

"Who knows—soon we may have the capacity to move all of our people to Planet Earth, where we can all be free to express our true intelligence," Caleb offered, swiftly returning to his workstation. All cheered again in agreement.

"You know what?" Lunar said, "we all deserve the night off. Gentlemen—go home to your wives and families. If you are single, find someone to celebrate this joyous occasion with."

The group cheered again. "Just remember to keep the reason for your joy a secret. We'll reconvene at first light."

"I will hug my wife a little tighter tonight," Caleb quipped, "I guarantee that she will be shocked out of her wits." Once again, the group erupted in laughter.

The crew had no knowledge of Akello's next visit. Very little to nothing was known about the plans he had for the Kingdom of Nuria. However, the Nurians intended to remedy their constriction by relocating to Planet Earth. It was quite evident that, given the odds, the Nurians will need to work swiftly and accurately. They could only hope that construction of the portal, and exodus of the Nurians to Earth, will be expediently achieved before the arrival of the Asterian intruders.

CHAPTER 15
KINGDOM SVANIA

"The Asterians are here!" some women shouted as they scurried about the main market of Svania. Persons peered about curiously, in efforts of spotting Akello and his men. Akello's visit had been anticipated since his ascension to chief. However, the slight chaos amongst the Svanian was not entirely due to his visit. A few yards away a gathering was making a fuss.

Aries, with the help of her cherolith, had managed to make the journey to the streets and now stood amidst the gathering that is openly rebuking both her and her pet.

"Don't think we don't recognize you, trickster!" one of the locals scowled, ensuring a safe distance between herself and the creature.

"No disguise today?" yelled another, taking a few more cautious steps backwards.

"I think she usually wears her disguises to avoid being recognized," offered another, her stance ready—just in case Aries released the creature.

"Today, she's pretending to be blind!" a few of the other women added scornfully.

The cherolith growled menacingly, scaring the women away.

Shunned and unable to see, Aries steadied her trembling hands on the head of her pet. "Good girl," she whispered, then wondered how she may successfully convince one of these women to be her personal assistant. An even greater concern was getting this done in time to be escorted to the citadel to plead with Ziva. Aries had overheard the announcement of the arrival of Akello. She felt that this had directed much attention away from her, and fortunately preoccupied most, giving her a moment to gather her thoughts.

"That's a loathsome-looking pet you have there," someone remarked.

Aries turned her head in the direction of the feminine voice. "Excuse me?" she said, hoping that fate had stepped in to aid her.

"The creature you have there …"

"She's a cherolith," Aries replied defensively, "she's the last of her kind actually. She was given to me as a gift."

"Really? That's a she?"

"Yes."

"Was she gifted to you before or after you tricked the previous owner?" the woman asked mockingly.

"Who are you?" Aries asked, her words dripping with curiosity. She heard her cherolith growl.

"Careful there, creature," the woman warned the pet sternly. "You're no match for me," she cooed.

"Wait, who are you?"

"I am snoopy," the woman replied.

"Snoopy as in, being nosy?" Aries quizzed, baffled.

"Of course not," the woman chuckled. "Snoopy as in, being interested," she clarified.

"Are you sure you wish to keep testing me?" Aries asked, frustrated. If she'd still possessed her gift of sight, she would have found a way to teach this woman a lesson.

As if she could read Aries' thoughts, she said, "Ziva bade me here."

"Ziva sent you to me?" Aries asked, even more taken aback.

"Yes, he has," the woman replied mockingly.

"Why?"

"Why indeed," the woman quipped. "I was directed by Ziva to step in—and help you in your time of need. I'm here to be your guide."

"My guide?" Aries felt her heart racing, as the hair on the back of her neck stood up. She realized she was face to face with a mysterious being that had been summoned to her by Ziva. Her pet continued to growl.

"Going forward, I'll be your eyes and ears," the woman said. But Aries understood this to be false. There was something ghastly and other-worldly about the woman.

"Why so sullen?" the woman asked, jolting Aries from her thoughts. "Cheer up. A very handsome young chief is making his way over to you as we speak."

"I need to go." Aries spun, steering her immense pet in the opposite direction of the woman's voice. She was now strongly doubtful of ever getting a chance to personally meet with Ziva. The sudden emergence of this strange woman had ruined any motivation for any such visit.

"What creature is this?" a male voice greeted cheerfully, thwarting Aries' efforts of escaping her mysterious stalker.

"It's a cherolith," the woman offered hastily. "The last of its kind, Chief Akello" she offered, her tone filled with tease.

"Thanks for speaking on my behalf—what did you say your name was again?" Aries replied sarcastically, slanting her neck in anticipation of a response. But the woman did not respond.

"Qarhan, have you ever seen such a shocking creature?" Akello continued boldly.

Aries' heart accelerated as she now recognized the man's voice from her vision. He's the man she had been fated to love. Ostracized from society, she had never seen Akello's face; and as fate would have it, she still could not see his face, though he was standing right in front of her. He was the man from her vision!

"This creature certainly is distinct," Qarhan replied vaguely.

"Interesting choice of pet, for such a beautiful damsel," Akello beamed at Aries.

"I suppose you're referring to me," Aries reasoned nervously. She wondered what would become of her on this day. She understood that Ziva had stolen her gift, but she remained slightly baffled as to why visions of days ahead evaded her. Afterall, before she had lost her sight, she had a vision of meeting the man who now stood in front of her—while she is blind. So why had visions of days ahead eluded her? Why did it stop at this day? Would she die before the day was over?

"Are you with us, my dear?" Akello's councilmen asked, interrupting her thoughts.

"Oh, uh, I'm so sorry. I must confess; I recently lost my ability to see—I'm so overwhelmed. I have many things on my mind." The sudden silence was deafening, so Aries continued coyly. "My name is Aries. This woman here has just informed me that Ziva is the cause of my demise, and he has sent her here to see to it that I remain punished," Aries explained.

"How dare you!" the woman yelled. "She's the perilous trickster that many have told you about, Akello. You must not listen to a word she says."

"Then, explain to us your purpose here!" Akello commanded.

"I owe you no such explana…"

"Her name is Mystique," Wizard Qarhan interrupted. I discerned that that she is a mystical being, summoned by Ziva to execute an unknown mission."

"Can you discern what that unknown mission is?" Akello asked.

"I cannot," Qarhan replied, "But Ziva can be rather—childish. Surely, my irrefutable powers far exceed Ziva's inconsequential tricks," Qarhan said defensively.

"It is hardly an inconsequential trick if you are unable to replicate it," Akello snapped at him.

"Is your name Mystique?" A council member asked the woman.

"Perhaps you should listen to your wizard," the woman hissed.

"Tell you what, lady of mystery," Akello spoke again, "you are free to go. I'd like to take a moment to fraternize with Aries," he said rationally. Aries' protective stance mellowed as Akello's rich confidence soothed her. She dismissed her thoughts of why Ziva's intrusion spell had not deflected both her and Akello's romantic charge.

"I go wherever Aries goes," the woman hissed again. The men gasped, feeling a bit frightened. Fear engulfed Aries once more.

"Very well then," Akello replied easily, "my men and I were on our way to visit Ziva. Will you join us?" Akello offered Aries who is completely stunned by the turn of events. Hadn't that been her purpose for setting out this day?

"Sure," she answered, almost breathless from both shock and fear. Akello guided Aries' arm through his. The cherolith growled.

"Easy girl," Aries whispered, quieting the beast.

"You are fascinating," Akello beamed at Aries. He then kissed her palm. Aries felt the earth move. There was something electric about Akello. She didn't have to see him to know that he was fetching. Something deep inside was telling her that the lifeforce must have once again been compromised if the intrusion spell no longer worked. She knew that the intrusion spell was no longer active because she and Akello were clearly smitten by each other. Aries' lips slightly parted into a smile. If the lifeforce was compromised, then her vision might return along with her gift, and the other powers she once experienced when the lifeforce had been down. Nevertheless, she continued her journey to the citadel with the group. She was curious to see what interesting events were about to unfold.

As they made their way to see the wizard, so did Mystique.

"Why is she tailing us?" Akello whispered to Wizard Qarhan.

"She's tailing Aries, not us," Qarhan explained.

"So, she is whom you said she was?" Akello quizzed.

"I'm sure of it," Qarhan replied.

"You must find a way to get rid of her," Akello advised.

"I'll know more once we speak to Ziva," Qarhan assured, averting Akello's dissatisfied gaze.

"My lovely Aries, tell me more about your pet—and how you have come to be known as a perilous trickster," Akello said, removing his gaze from Qarhan and smiling wickedly at the damsel he escorted. Akello considered how his men had been doing a great job at hiding their excitement about this particular trip to Svania—even the mere fact that he'd been able to flirt so easily with Aries.

"With pleasure," Aries smiled charmingly, as she began her spiel. She open-heartedly welcomed the delightful companionships, particularly Akello's. However, there was something else amidst that Aries had been inwardly welcoming of. It was the return of her sight. While the men secretly fantasized about the lifting of the intrusion spell, Aries secretly perceived light and frames of different images. Her eyesight was returning. She knew this could possibly mean that Ziva and the lifeforce were both gone. But perhaps it could also mean that Ziva had simply just lifted the spell. There was no rush, however, in announcing the good news. At least not until she was sure of Ziva's whereabouts and had solidified her friendship with Akello. What an amazing ally he would make. Thoughts of Ziva's absence danced about in Aries' mind. Without a lifeforce to rule the realm, Aries could ascend to ruler.

CHAPTER 16
KINGDOM OCTUSHI: THE DESOLATE LAND

Wizard Ziva had been trapped in Kingdom Octushi. He had awakened from a deep sleep, shocked at the realization of still being alive. He scanned his surroundings for signs of life, or light, or anything, but the only visibility was vast starkness. His portal had completely dried up, and not an ounce of magic could be summoned. He attempted to stand, but his weakened legs gave way. He fell back down onto the dusty bare ground. Unable to discern the power of the water-force, Ziva cleared his parched throat, preparing to shout for help. Just as he was about to yell, a voice boomed round about him.

"Ziva, you're awake," the voice said.

"Who's there?" Ziva asked, startled. He whirled about the ground briskly, trying to locate the source of the sound.

"How are you feeling? You must be thirsty." the voice urged.

"Show yourself!" Ziva yelled.

"Alright, if you insist," the voice said.

A dark, male silhouette suddenly appeared in front of Ziva.

"I asked you to show yourself," Ziva insisted.

"I am showing myself. This, is me, and I am pleased to meet your acquaintance."

"If this is you—then what are you?"

"I am Shadow, lifeforce of this kingdom."

"I beg your pardon?" Ziva said in bewilderment.

"Ziva, relax. Here, drink this." Shadow stretched forth his dark, silhouetted hand, motioning for Ziva to take the mug of water that had suddenly appeared before him.

"How did you do that—what are you?"

"You need to drink if you are to recoup your strength."

"How am I still alive? What are you? How long have I been-- out?"

"I'll tell you all you need to know after you've had your drink."

Ziva cautiously retrieved the mug and reluctantly took his first sip. The surprisingly flavorful taste slowly awakened his energy and refreshed him. Before long, he had downed the entire contents, sating his parched insides.

"Excellent!" Shadow exclaimed, seemingly pleased at how smooth the encounter was progressing—so far. "Now let me explain. I am Shadow. I embody the lifeforce of this kingdom."

"What does that even mean? Octushi has always been a desolate land—no lifeforce exists here." Replied Ziva.

"Never have I revealed my existence to anyone—as there was no need to," Shadow explained.

"I don't understand—how can you be the lifeforce of Octushi? No life exists in this kingdom. My kingdom, Svania, where I am from, has been the only kingdom with a lifeforce."

"Ziva, Kingdom Svania, where you are from, no longer has a lifeforce," Shadow explained.

"Meaning what? How do you even know my name?"

"Before your arrival, I existed, but was not triggered until the loss of your kingdom's lifeforce."

"Are you telling me my kingdom's lifeforce is gone—so the water-force is gone?"

"Yes."

"You're saying that—this has now activated you?" Ziva asked, stunned.

"Your kingdom's lifeforce is no more." Shadow confirmed, "and yes, I was dormant until this event awoke me."

"So—if the water-force is terminated—which would cause the lifeforce to also be terminated then—then how am I alive?"

"You're alive only by my choice," Shadow stated, watching Ziva's expression grow cold with disbelief.

"That's impossible," Ziva protested.

"Ziva, I'm sure that by now you've realized that your water-force counterpart had been right all along. You should have abandoned the dimension spell, but you didn't, and now you must live with the consequences, or die—the choice is yours," Shadow explained.

"How can you possibly know all of this?" Ziva asked.

"Simple. I have acquired the essence of your water-force," Shadow retorted.

"This must be a dream—none of this is real! I must still be dying," Ziva muttered to himself. "The elixir—this must be the effects of the elixir," he continued, crazedly feeling about himself for who-knows-what.

"Forget about the elixir, Ziva. Calm down and listen to me because it is important that you do. I am real—all of this is real. Kingdom Octushi is real, and you are stuck here with me now."

Paralyzed by grief and horror, Wizard Ziva willed his mind to be calm. Shadow did have a point. Ziva would no longer feel the energy of the water-force pulsating through him, which could only mean that there was no more water-force, and thus, no more lifeforce. Ziva realized he was stuck in Octushi, with a terrifying, faceless being, Shadow, who has essentially swallowed the water-force, which was Ziva's other half. Ziva wondered how he could have been so erroneous to have worked against his own lifeforce. These actions were not only unnatural, but also gravely disingenuous. As Shadow continued, Ziva felt his heart sinking deeper and deeper into a dark void now within him. A thought suddenly occurred to Ziva. If this Shadow-being has swallowed the water-force which was his other half, why was it keeping Ziva alive?

"Ziva, are you listening to me?" Shadow asked. Ziva was jolted from his thoughts.

"I am listening," Ziva confirmed with a deep sigh.

"Very good. Like I was saying, similar to your prior situation where your existence was tied to the water-force, and you both made up the lifeforce which was tied to Kingdom Svania, my existence is tied to Kingdom Octushi," Shadow explained.

"I see," said Ziva pensively.

Shadow continued: "As you may already be aware, your absence from your kingdom has severed your ties with your water-force, thus ultimately severing your ties with your kingdom's lifeforce, thus voiding you and your lifeforce. Do you understand this?"

"Not completely," Ziva muttered beneath his breath. "If I've been voided—how am I still alive?"

"You're alive because of me. When I acquired your water-force, I was able to use that essence to breathe life back into you temporarily—a continued life for you would only be contingent upon your acceptance of an offer I have for you."

"Oh, I see. So, you're only keeping me alive to see if I'll accept an offer from you. Quite some offer that must be." Ziva gulped.

"Indeed," Shadow said, as if amused.

"What is this offer?" Ziva asked, feeling completely overwhelmed.

"In exchange for continued life, you will allow me to acquire your body." Shadow offered.

"And there it is!" Ziva spat. "You who have acquired my water-force, the other half of me, now seek to be my parasite!" Ziva gasped.

"Hardly," Shadow shrugged. "On the contrary, I only wish to share a mutually beneficial relationship with you. You would become the face of my being, and in return, you'd have unlimited access to my powers."

"Given all your powers, why do you need my body? Why don't you go out and find someone else for your exploits?" Ziva asked.

"Ziva, this is a tremendous opportunity that I am granting you. I need your spoken acceptance of my offer immediately, otherwise you die." Shadow warned.

"An opportunity?" Ziva scoffed. "You need me to willingly sell my soul to you to stay alive. I decline this offer."

"The only way for this to work is through your spoken acceptance; otherwise, you die. Either way, I continue to exist, so suit yourself."

"Then I choose to die," Ziva scowled.

"Think about what you are giving up, Ziva. If we bonded, we could gain power enough to rule over the entire realm. You would get your kingdom back—and rule without a water-force. You'd gain the ability to naturally teleport—without a dimension spell. You would still be you, and I would merely exist within you. We would co-exist synergistically, and be a force to be reckoned with, and the best part? You'd no longer have any ties to contend with."

"Indeed. I'd just have you to contend with instead." Ziva's tone dripped with sarcasm.

"But we would exist as one entity—as a whole, instead of two separate entities, as you did previously."

Ziva's heart and mind raced simultaneously. He realized that his impending death, which Shadow constantly referenced, was now at hand. Ziva felt himself slowly drifting away from all existence, again. He closed his eyes and let go, allowing himself to drift away from all that existed.

CHAPTER 17
KINGDOM OCTUSHI

"Wake up!" Shadow commanded. Once again, Ziva rose from his slumber, devastated at the realization of still being alive. It was now evident that this entity—this Shadow, had no intention of letting him go.

"You plan on keeping me alive until you bend me to your will," Ziva gasped in horror. "That's why you won't let me die. I thought you said the choice was mine ..."

"Enough!" Shadow interjected. He was growing impatient.

"You have stalled for longer than I anticipated. In so doing, you have cost me crucial time." Shadow roared. At the sound of Shadow's voice, thunder boomed in the distance, and glimmers of lightning flashed across Octushi's gloomy horizons. It was now very clear that Shadow was uniquely powerful, and this sudden clarity terrified Ziva.

"Why the sudden impatience? What's your rush?" Ziva inquired.

"Have you reconsidered my offer?" Shadow asked urgently. "You'll gain a better perspective once we synchronize."

"Synchronize? You're hoping that I'll hand over to you the little of me that's left, despite your lack of transparency?"

"Nonsense! I've been very transparent with you. I've told you everything you need to know! You'll gain a much better understanding of things once we fuse our essences."

"Once again, I decline your offer, Shadow. Go and find someone else to deceive and exploit. You've already ripped my kingdom from me."

"And you have yourself to blame for that. The water-force had warned you against a dimension spell. You were also warned about Aries."

"What I just can't understand is how my dimension spell could have caused all of this. Furthermore, what does any of this have to do with Aries? Instead of just piggybacking off the memories of my water-force, you should be admitting that Wizard Qarhan of Asteria is the one responsible for..." Ziva's voice trailed off as a new thought occurred to him.

"Wait just a moment!" he suddenly exclaimed. "Shadow, you're the one who's responsible for this."

"Nonsense!" Shadow said defensively. "Do not blame me for your predicament, Ziva. I'm just simply providing you with a perfect solution to your problem."

"Turning myself over to you is not a solution."

"You don't trust me, is that it?" asked Shadow.

"How can anyone trust you? Shadow, you appear to be hiding valuable information that I so desperately need. I will never ..."

"Alright then," Shadow grimaced, cutting Ziva off. "Let's have a look," he continued, holding out his silhouetted hand to Ziva. Shadow opened his palm to expose what appeared to be a small, glowing jewel.

"What's that?" asked Ziva.

"This, dear wizard, is my rudenium stone."

"Rudenium?"

"It is ruthenium combined with ancient archetypal magic to give us rudenium."

"And what is this supposed to do?" Ziva eyed the stone skeptically.

"This is how I see what goes on within the other kingdoms."

"Oh?" Ziva retrieved the stone from Shadow's palm and inspected it. "Seems like a regular shiny stone to me."

"Look deeper," Shadow urged, observing as Ziva's expression lit up as images came to life within the stone's glow.

"Fascinating," said Ziva. "But I've been a wizard for hundreds of years. Why have I no knowledge of such an enchanted stone?"

"I assure you, as a once-dormant but older lifeforce nonetheless, there's much knowledge that you have not been made privy to. Rare types of enchantments do exist in this universe, that only rare types of lifeforces know of."

"So, you're trying to say that you're a rare type of lifeforce," Ziva's tone dripped with cynicism.

"I wouldn't say that I am just yet."

"When would you say it? Oh—let me guess. You wish to wait until I surrender my existence over to you."

"Ziva, pay attention to the images inside the stone's glow. Tell me what you see," instructed Shadow, clearly beyond agitated. Ziva was becoming a tougher stone to crack than expected.

"I see—I see Svania, my kingdom! That is the marketplace, and those are my people. They're alive!" Ziva gasped, shocked at the images. "What manner of enchantment is this?"

"I was granted the unique gift to wield the power of the rudenium stone." Shadow explained. "Which is how I was able to confirm that the water-force's suspicions about Aries were true. Let's shift kingdoms so you can see what the Nurians have been up to." Shadow glided his palm over the stone that now nestled in Ziva's opened palm. The colors from the glow changed and the scene within it shifted to images of Nuria.

"Nuria, just as I remembered it," inhaled Ziva. "I recall looking down at the kingdom from atop the rays of its corona when my portal had malfunctioned there. "Yes! There is the cell in which I was held captive but only for a short while."

Shadow motioned his palm over the stone once again and the images shifted to reveal the Nurians embarking a portal.

"I should have known that this was trickery!" Ziva spat. "Just a mere sleight of hand. The Nurians are a people of intellect. They have no magic!"

"Ziva, this is your last time suggesting I'm dishonest."

"But how can the Nurians be boarding a portal without magic? Is Wizard Qarhan on board the portal?"

"No, he's not. The Nurians have used their masterfully hidden intellect to reverse engineer your portal from remnants you left behind." Shadow said snidely, emphasizing the words, "your" and "portal."

This information came as another devastating blow to Ziva. He wondered how such a thing could be possible without a spell.

"Why are they leaving—and so what, if they do?" Ziva stuttered in shock.

"The forces have been dispensed such that all inhabitants abide within the kingdoms of Zannus, otherwise the entire realm will collapse."

"So that would mean that we are all tied to our kingdoms, and you are tied to this kingdom, which is why you haven't used your unique powers to leave Octushi and find yourself another body to occupy," Ziva's own words shocked him. He was stunned by his own revelation.

"Not quite," Shadow began to pace about.

"So, I'm right," exclaimed Ziva.

"Not completely," Shadow repeated. "Ok, fine. While we may not all be tied to our designated kingdoms, we are all tied to Zannus Realm." Shadow paused.

"Continue," Ziva urged.

"As lifeforce of Svania, you were tied to the kingdom. Just as I am tied to this kingdom as the lifeforce of Octushi. Your people are alive and well, despite your collapse, but without a replacement lifeforce, they will disintegrate, consequently risking the entire realm." Shadow paused again.

"I'm listening," Ziva urged.

"The people of Kingdoms Nuria and Asteria are not overseen by lifeforces, and are therefore not tied to their kingdoms, thus their capacity to wander about unharmed. However, their prolonged absence from the realm could cause it's collapse."

"Then someone needs to fetch the people of Nuria before they are lost to Zannus Realm!"

"Thus, my reason for the opportunity I've been trying to grant you."

"Uh-huh."

"Ziva, without me, your existence is over. Accepting my offer would free both of us from our ties. You would have your kingdom back and could rule more powerfully. You would gain access to not just my powers, but your water-force's as well. Most importantly, we could possibly retrieve the people of Nuria before they are lost to the realm."

"What if we fuse our essences, but fail at retrieving the Nurians? Wouldn't we all eventually perish? Of what use would our fusion be then?"

"I'm sure that through the strength of our combined powers, we could work something out. Let us cross that bridge if and when we get there."

"I see," Ziva muttered in deep consideration. "Are you sure that you—I mean we—would no longer be stuck here in Octushi?" He closed his palm over the stone which, by now, had stopped glowing with its dynamic images.

"We would no longer be stuck here. I'm sure of it. It's a splendid coincidence that you ended up here in Octushi when you did," Shadow motioned for Ziva to return the rudenium stone to him.

"Hmm," grunted Ziva, returning the stone to Shadow. Moments later, the stone vanished from Shadow's palm.

"There's something else you need to know."

"There's more?"

"Yes, Aries is what's called an archetypal being."

"Meaning?"

"Meaning she is meant to be a great and powerful lifeforce. The rarest kind, possibly one of the greatest that ever existed."

"And you call yourself honest?"

"I am being honest, Ziva. You're walking a thin line."

"Aries is a commoner. She's a trickster who uses her gift of foresight against her own people and to her sole benefit."

"Where do you think such a gift comes from?" Shadow asked. He waited for a response, then continued when he received none from his highly distraught guest. "Aries is not yet aware of her origin. She believes herself to be a mere human—a seer. She operates within the confines of such a belief, as the ancient great forces designed it to be. Ziva, you need to understand something. Aries had initiated the idea of the dimension spell for a reason."

"What reason is that?"

"She perceived that the idea would get us to where we are now."

"In a situation where our kingdom's lifeforce is destroyed?"

"Exactly."

"But what good is it that she would see her own kingdom's lifeforce destroyed? Is she pure evil? What could have compelled her to initiate such an idea?"

"Whether she's pure evil is yet to be seen. I don't think she has figured out all the details yet. But what I do know is that forces within the universe have shifted, thus allowing Aries to be compelled by her own subconscious." Shadow explained. Ziva shook his head.

"Nonsense!"

"I understand that you're confused," Shadow continued. "Aries is beginning to come into her own. Like me, she is a lifeforce. But unlike me, she could become far more powerful. She could transition into what is known as an archetypal lifeforce. Until recently, she'd been blissfully unaware of her truth, and existed in this manner to maintain balances within the forcefields of this universe. Now that Svania's lifeforce has diminished, Aries' powers have gradually increased, and will continue to do so until she has fully transformed into her true self. Very soon she could become powerful enough to either rule over realms or destroy them. She poses a great threat to all of Zannus, because her gift of vision—foresight as you call it, could increase enough to allow her to foresee all things within our realm, and perceive the goings-on of each kingdom. If you allow me to sync essences with you, we could become powerful enough to weaken her by taking her gift of vision, and ultimately subduing her altogether before she fully acclimates to all of her powers." Shadow concluded.

"But you need to possess my body first—and I must agree. I must verbalize my agreement for the possession to be binding." Ziva now understood Shadow's offer, which now seemed reasonable enough. Furthermore, what lifeforce would wish to remain tied to a desolate kingdom, existing as a mere ghost? His powers would essentially go unused, and his existence would be purposeless. Shadow had been laying around dormant for centuries, until his recent awakening. A lifeforce must exist within the realm to prevent the realm's ultimate collapse, and the people of Nuria must be retrieved to also prevent the realm's ultimate collapse.

Now that the prior lifeforce had collapsed, Shadow's powers were now awakened, and he was ready to abandon his existence as a mere shadow. Ziva contemplated his newfound knowledge of Aries archetypal situation. He wondered how this was even possible. Ziva realized that accepting Shadow's offer might not be such a bad idea after all. There was great work to be done. Instead of dying, he might even have a chance at outmaneuvering both Shadow and Aries—that is if Aries even posed any sort of threat at all. He could ultimately become the lifeforce of Zannus realm. He highly doubted that Shadow spoke the whole truth, but most of what he'd learned seemed plausible enough.

"I accept," Ziva murmured dismally.

"Pardon?"

"You may acquire my body, so we may fuse our essences to exist as one, and rule the realm—together, as one" Ziva confirmed.

"Be aware that this is irreversible," cautioned Shadow.

"My mind is made up," Ziva said with certainty.

"Alright then," said Shadow, relieved. "We've already lost a lot of time, so I'll proceed with the ritual at once."

Shadow began his chant, muttering: *"Forces of Zannus Realm, bind me with this vessel,"* Shadow wasted no time inserting himself into Ziva's body. Ziva wailed as Shadow's entry seared through him. Ziva's eyes glowed as Shadow's mighty force penetrated him. The synchronization process had begun.

CHAPTER 18
Akello

Akello and his men arrived at the citadel, stunned to find all seven of Empress Senya's maidens restlessly pacing about the courtyard.

"Open the gates, lead maiden!" Serena, shouted. "Hurry, it's the Asterian Chief!" She beckoned for the gatekeeper to allow the troop in.

"Hello everyone," Akello greeted, "why so glum?" he asked.

"I hope I have addressed you correctly, Akello. You were slated to ascend to the role of chief when we last spoke with your father, Leo," Serena explained.

"You are correct as always, Serena." Akello smiled charmingly while noting his smile was not reciprocated. There was something rather peculiar about the women today.

"Congratulations, and welcome." Serena nodded in acknowledgment, while quickly glancing away to avert any eye contact with Aries, the seer.

"Thank you, Serena. Ladies, these gentlemen are my council members and guards; they constitute my team, serve as governors to the realm, and act as lead battalion, when necessary," Akello announced.

"Welcome!" the women chorused, throwing quick and uncomfortable glances over at Aries.

"This lady on my arm is Aries, and of course, the gentleman with the rod, you already know him to be our wizard. The lady behind him, we're not so sure about. Her name is Mystique and she is very obsessed with Aries." Akello explained as he concluded his introductions.

"Good to see you again, Qarhan," Serena greeted, purposefully ignoring the very peculiar-looking Mystique, as well as Aries, whom she had immediately recognized to be the conniving, calculating trickster that their society had ostracized.

"How may we help you?" Serena asked nervously.

"Just the usual visit," Akello stated casually.

"Oh, well, in that case, our lady Senya is currently indisposed."

"Is the lady alright?" Aries eagerly chimed in. She observed the searching exchange amongst the women. Her sight had officially returned, but she kept up pretenses to remain ahead of everyone.

Sensing the women's resentment towards Aries, Akello reiterated, "How is the Empress?"

"She hasn't been doing very well," Serena replied.

"What's going on?"

"We're not sure of what's going on—she just hasn't been herself lately."

"What about Wizard Ziva? Is he working to fix the problem?" Wizard Qarhan smirked, his sarcasm noted by all who were present. Chief Akello tried desperately to swallow his rage. He'd been all too familiar with the direction in which Qarhan was heading—always towards a path of unrequited competition with Wizard Ziva. Meanwhile, Aries' heart raced with excitement as she awaited Serena's response to Qarhan's question.

"I think that you'll be better off personally speaking with the empress about this," Serena finally said awkwardly. She quickly glanced around at the other ladies who nodded in agreement with her.

"Speak with me about what?" Empress Senya asked, suddenly approaching from behind and immediately locking gaze with Aries when everyone turned their attention to her. "I see that your vision has returned," Senya stated cynically, observing as a startled Aries quickly unlocked their gaze to look away. But it was too late—Aries had been discovered. She inwardly kicked herself for being caught off guard by Senya's sudden arrival. Aries blamed her reflexes.

"You're aware of her condition?" councilman eleven asked.

"I've been aware of it, but I can tell that she's no longer blind."

"What do you mean? I've lost my sight!" Aries shouted, now peering down at the ground.

"Then explain to us how you were able to look me right in the eyes just now," Senya challenged.

"I didn't look you in the eyes." After all, there was no way for Senya to prove that Aries was lying. Yet, Aries could feel trouble brewing. Senya's aura had changed. The empress had not seemed timid in revealing to everyone that she'd had prior knowledge of Aries' blindness. This was troubling for Aries. Had she foreseen such a troubling moment beforehand, she wouldn't have set out for the citadel in the first place.

"Chief Akello, is it?" Senya switched her focus to a very baffled Akello.

"Yes, I'm chief now," Akello replied.

"I see you've made friends with the kingdom's charlatan," Senya hissed.

"Such harsh words," Aries said desperately.

"We met her on our way here—interestingly, our stunning little charlatan here explained how she'd been misunderstood by everyone," Akello forced himself to say, while dismissing surges of awkwardness.

"Wizard Ziva is not here," Senya hissed. "Do you know why?" she asked Akello.

"Please, do tell," Akello encouraged casually, but deep down he was dying to know once and for all the truth about what was going on.

Wizard Qarhan, the guards, the councilmen and Mystique cocked their ears, eagerly waiting for Senya's spiel. Aries on the other hand, wished for the opposite. In that moment, she no longer cared to know of Ziva's whereabouts. Instead, she secretly wished for Senya's silence. How much of their secret did Senya plan to dispel to the gathering? This was all happening at the wrong time. Aries felt that she had clearly managed to get rid of one wizard, only to fall into the midst of another, Wizard Qarhan. Worst of all, her rapport with Akello was about to shatter. Her only means of defense was to lie her way out of the predicament. Regroup. Return.

"Aries tricked him," Senya hissed.

"Wait! What?" Aries said, bewildered. The rest of the group gasped in disbelief.

"That's right, the woman you have so lovingly locked arms with, has tricked Wizard Ziva into performing a spell that would potentially hurt our entire kingdom," Senya announced as she glared at Aries. But Aries kept her gaze affixed to the ground, stunned by Senya's cleverness.

"So, what you're telling us," Qarhan chimed, "is that your wizard, Ziva, fell for the trick of a common citizen, consequently risking his entire kingdom. Is this correct?" he asked, smirking and refusing to meet Akello's glare.

"Correct," Senya confirmed.

"I'm sure there must be an explanation for all of this," Akello said, forcing a smile. He glanced over at Aries and asked, "Are you able to corroborate any of the charges being brought against you?"

"Charges?" Aries exclaimed. The cherolith broke its silence and began to growl. "These are hardly charges. These are all lies."

"Lies or not, Aries, your empress' complaints cannot go unheeded." He released her from his arm and signaled for Qarhan to draw closer. "Qarhan, I need you to tell us whether Aries is blind," he whispered into Qarhan's ear.

"You know that I'm blind. You saw it yourself. Mystique has even admitted it to you. What further proof do you need? You have to believe me," Aries pleaded in efforts of deterring the inevitable.

"Qarhan," Akello said, nodding.

Qarhan gently placed a palm over Aries' eyes and paused a moment.

"She is not blind," Qarhan confirmed, "I have discerned it."

The small crowd gasped again in horror.

"You made us all believe that you are blind!" Akello scowled, stepping away from Aries.

"Now you see why she's known as the trickster." Aries smiled wickedly.

"I was blind!" Aries finally looked up at them. "But I regained my vision on the way here. I was afraid of sharing the news and wanted to wait until I see Ziva first."

"Aha!" Senya chuckled drily, "so you tricked the high chief into getting you through our gates to find out whether Ziva has recovered from your trick. Akello, why don't you ask her why she wishes to see Ziva?"

Akello felt his fantasy of Aries take flight. "Senya, tell you what, let me speak privately with you and Ziva so we can figure this out together."

"Ziva has not yet arrived," Senya said with swiftness. She had no intentions of revealing to Akello that her kingdom might have lost its wizard, and thus its lifeforce. Additionally, it didn't appear to Senya that Aries could perceive Ziva's whereabouts, so she hoped that this moment might be her best chance to justifiably rid her kingdom of Aries. "Put the trickster in the

"Wait--what?" Aries said, shocked.

"Akello, please have your men put Aries in the dungeon," Senya repeated.

"I can assure you that that will not be necessary," Akello intervened. "I believe Ziva might have already remedied the situation by summoning Mystique to keep an eye on Aries."

"Mystique?" Senya echoed.

"Yes, Qarhan discerns Mystique to have been summoned by Ziva to tail Aries—I think it's starting to add up now."

"So, where was Mystique when Aries tricked you about being blind?" Senya argued.

"She was blind! Ziva sent me after he rendered her sightless," Mystique said. Aries felt grateful to Mystique for the glimmer of hope.

"Well now, Mystique, you are welcome to join Aries in the dungeon," Senya said, crushing that glimmer of hope.

"There has to be another way," Akello insisted.

"Would you put me and my people at risk by setting her free?" Senya snapped at him.

"We wouldn't dare to do that," councilman eleven quickly interjected. "But given that she's operated freely all this time when she was up to no good, why don't we just hold her temporarily instead, until Ziva returns to the citadel to sort all of this?"

Senya seemed pleased by this recommendation. Aries scowled at her knowingly.

"There! Nothing like an intelligent brainstorm," Akello said. "Councilmen six and eleven, take one of my soldiers and escort Aries and Mystique to the holding area."

"Serena, please show these gentlemen the way," Senya said.

"Gentlemen, follow me," Serena said, leading them into the citadel, while cautiously avoiding the growling beast.

Akello's mind was racing. He was completely smitten by Aries and wondered how things could have gone so wrong so quickly. Though she'd disappointed him, he was saddened to see things go so badly for Aries. There must be a way to contact Wizard Ziva—get to the bottom of this, fix things, carry out his mission, and achieve his goals. He gestured for Qarhan to step closer.

"I need you to use your powers to locate Ziva," Akello instructed matter-of-factly.

"That's not possible," Qarhan countered.

"That's why I need you to do it."

"I cannot do it."

"Why not?"

"Because it's impossible."

"Qarhan..." Akello said through gritted teeth.

"I sense that something has gone terribly wrong here, as I no longer sense this kingdom's magic."

"What do you mean?" Akello whispered.

"I have not been able to discern Ziva's nor the water-force's presence. I sense that even their fountain of life has dried up."

"Are you sure of what you're saying?" Akello asked, bewildered.

"Yes, I sensed this after overhearing whispers among the maidens."

"Can you sense Ziva's location?"

"I'm unable to at this time."

"Well, can you beam me back to Asteria? Is this something you think you're able to do?"

"We're leaving?"

"No, just you and me."

"I thought we were waiting for Ziva to return."

"Return from where?"

"I don't know …"

"Exactly, Qarhan. You don't know. I urgently need to speak with father. You'll escort me through the portal. We'll return once I've spoken to father. Is this something that is feasible for you?"

"Yes, it is."

"Gentlemen, Qarhan is taking me back to Asteria for an impromptu meeting. You may continue to wait at the citadel for Ziva—I shall return shortly."

"Wait a minute," councilman two shouted, "you're not about to sneak off and have all the fun, are you?" he winked.

"Not until after we've met with Ziva," Akello responded with a wink.

"My maidens will keep you entertained," Senya said, gesturing at the ladies who had been curiously observing her. They knew she was hiding something but dared not demand the truth.

"Gentlemen, follow us," the ladies instructed, leading the men away.

"Until we meet up again," Senya said, sashaying out the exit.

Moments later, Qarhan conjured the portal and departed with Akello to Kingdom Asteria.

CHAPTER 19
Akello

Chief Akello resisted the urge to hug his father. "How is mother?" he asked. His father did not respond. "I'm sorry we're at odds, father," he admitted.

They stood in silence for a moment longer and then Akello asked, "Father, do you think that there is something wrong with Wizard Qarhan?"

"Be careful of what you say," his father cautioned, whispering. "You have blasphemed enough—furthermore, he could be somewhere listening, and that would be very dangerous for us both."

"Dangerous?" Akello whispered back. "I don't believe he has the power to listen in on us. Also—I don't even think that Qarhan is dangerous at all."

"What are you talking about?" Leo questioned.

"I'm seriously concerned that he's unable to fulfill most of my biddings. He consistently makes excuses for his failures, he seems to be hiding something, and he blames the wizard of Svania for executing unbreakable spells," Akello informed.

"Who can say for sure whether a spell is unbreakable or not?" his father asked.

Akello was taken aback.

"I don't know the answer to that," he said, "but my common sense and observation tells me there's something strange about our wizard. For instance, during our visit to Svania, he told me that he sensed that the lifeforce was gone."

"What lifeforce?" Leo boomed.

"The lifeforce of kingdom Svania."

"Hmm—have you spoken with Wizard Ziva about this?"

"No, Ziva is nowhere to be found."

"Meaning what? Has the wizard just upped and vanished from his own kingdom?"

"It appears so, father—even the empress, Senya, seems extremely worried about the wizard's disappearance."

"Is that so? And all of these strange occurrences have begun the moment you announced your blasphemous intentions for your rule within this realm ..."

"I can assure you that these peculiarities have nothing to do with my ..."

"Where is Wizard Qarhan?"

"I left him by the port ..."

"I need Qarhan to find a way to remove you from our government."

"Wait! What?"

"You have been a disgrace to my legacy for long enough ..."

"Father—how can you be so obstinate?"

"Qarhan is far more powerful than you think," Leo murmured, "If Wizard Ziva is truly missing, then Qarhan might replace him—assume his powers. So... be careful. Either you fall in line quickly, or prepare for the consequences ahead, Akello," Leo warned before storming off.

Akello watched longingly as his father strode away. He missed his father terribly and wished that things could just return to the way they were before. But that moment was fleeting. Akello hurried back to the port where Qarhan awaited his return. In efforts of burying the pain of a severed bond with his father, Akello allowed his mind to wander back to thoughts of Qarhan.

Akello spent most of his life visualizing himself with Wizard Qarhan by his side—forces to be reckoned with. Even the very goals that Akello had so carefully cultivated were mostly based on his confidence in Qarhan's magical abilities. On occasion, Akello had even secretly resented his father for not having put Qarhan to greater use, leading Akello to aspire to one day become all the great things his father had refused to be. Now this.

"There you are!" Qarhan greeted, disrupting Akello from his thoughts as he approached.

"From that worrisome look on your face, I gather that things did not go so well with your father."

"You are right," Akello replied flatly. "Father is still as angry with me."

"Things will brighten once we return to Svania with the others. You'll see." Qarhan smiled and motioned for Akello to step inside of the portal ahead of him.

Wizard Qarhan reflected on how he'd been curious as to the cause for Akello's impromptu return to Asteria. When Akello insisted that Qarhan wait for him by the Port, Qarhan had eagerly agreed and seated himself at a comfortable spot by the waterway. Qarhan had closed his eyes and mumbled a quick chant. Within moments Qarhan had left his body, sailed through the air, and caught up with Akello. Wizard Qarhan had been right there, the whole time, listening in on the conversation between current chief and predecessor, and it wasn't his first time doing this. Qarhan had used this ability as a way of gaining better insight into the type of people to which he'd been bound. Of the entire realm, Wizard Qarhan despised Akello the most, and secretly romanticized the destruction of the young leader's reign. He secretly contemplated abandoning the laws of the ancient lifeforces, to join efforts with Leo to remove the young chief from their government.

"We're in Svania again," Qarhan said, shifting from his thoughts. Akello stepped out of the portal and made his way with Qarhan back to the citadel to reconvene with the others.

CHAPTER 20
Aries: "The Talisman"

Aries the Seer had been carefully deposited into an isolated chamber situated beneath ground level of the citadel. She'd been locked away at Senya's bidding with promises of provisions of comfort from the councilmen. No amount of comfort was enough to offset the injustice she was experiencing. Aries felt that those whom she least expected had completely shattered her dignity. She settled on her decision for revenge.

Tears stung her eyes as she furiously scanned the cold, bland room. A cot in a corner boasted a dusty white sheet. Across the room was a small round table with a wooden bench. A modest pail of fresh water sat next to the entryway of a passage that led to what Aries presumed to be the restroom. She surmised the other cells within the prison had passageways that led to said restroom.

"You're the only prisoner here," Mystique offered.

"Be quiet!" Aries snapped, longing to be left alone with her thoughts. She wondered how long before this being dissipated, given that it's summoner no longer existed. Furthermore, she'd already perceived that she was alone with Mystique in the dungeon. She needed to devise a plan quickly but wondered if it was humanly possible at this point, to concoct the type of plan through which she could satisfactorily reconcile her predicament. Not only had she been relegated to the confines of a dungeon with a mystical being for sole companionship, her cherolith had been mistreated and confiscated as well.

"What's on your mind?" Mystique asked.

"Why? Does your mystical aura not allow you to read minds?" Aries hissed crossly. She wiped away a tear, walked over to the pail across the room, splashed water on her face, then closed her eyes and wondered how she might rid herself of Mystique. Moments later, she opened her eyes to see Mystique sauntering over to the bench and table on the other side of the room. Good.

Aries ventured over to the cot and seated herself with her back leaned against the wall. She closed her eyes again, in efforts of conjuring visions of the future. Now that her sight had returned, her ability to foresee the future would have likely returned with it. She perceived that Ziva had somehow connected both elements in his dream spell. Given that she could no longer perceive the lifeforce, she was convinced that it was no more, and all Ziva's spells would eventually become undone. Once again, she tried to summon visions of a future beyond this day but failed miserably. She wondered about Ziva, realizing there's something in her discernment of the wizard that did not match the complete void she felt when she considered the water-force. How was she able to still perceive Ziva to an extent, but not the water-force?

Aries decided to start at the beginning, in efforts of catching something—anything she might have previously missed. Prior to becoming sightless, she'd been unable to foresee a future beyond this day. She'd assumed this was due to her blindness, but deduced she'd been wrong about that. Her vision of meeting and falling in love with Akello, in the market, had come true while she was still blind. Therefore, if she was blind when she met Akello earlier that day, and her gift had enabled her to foresee that event anyway;

blindness could not have been the cause of the disruption of her abilities. In fact, though she had now regained her sight, she was still unable to foresee that which was to come. *So, what had changed? What had she missed?*

Hit by a dangerous realization, Aries suddenly popped her eyes wide open, and stared over at Mystique in bewilderment. Fortunately for Aries, Mystique was sitting in a most peculiar position facing the wall with her back turned. Mystique did not see Aries approaching. Aries reasoned that Mystique had been summoned by Ziva's magic. If the lifeforce had died, then what was Mystique still doing there with her in the dungeon—when so many of Ziva's greatest enchantments had already come undone? Her discernment of Ziva was that he still lived while the lifeforce was dead. Yet, she was positive that this was impossible. Fueled by a sudden surge of massive power from within, Aries ceased the opportunity to clench Mystique. She sprang across the table and quickly threw her arms around Mystique, engulfing her in a mighty embrace. Startled, Mystique shifted vigorously to free herself from Aries, but it was too late. She was already locked into Aries' grip, and Aries was already locked into a trance, using Mystique as a talisman to locate and connect with Ziva.

CHAPTER 21
Ziva: "I've Found You"

The symbiotic process between Ziva and Shadow had already begun. Although both beings continued to acclimate to each other, Ziva perceived the process to be almost completed. The progression so far, had been seamless, and though Shadow was the dominant force, the merging of the two existences had been far more harmonious than Ziva anticipated. Ziva could now perceive the intentions and desires of Shadow and even reason with Shadow—which was also himself—to mutually agree on decisions. Ziva now experienced a power beyond his wildest imagination, and slightly regretted his initial hesitation regarding the merger.

Ziva found it ironic that his name which stood for brilliance and light, completely contrasted with the dark entity seeking possession of him. Quite Ironic indeed. Ziva was now able to access Shadow's gift of wielding the power of the rudenium stone, to gain insight on many things, including the escape activities of the Nurians. He was also able to perceive the truth about Aries. He desired to tune in on Aries to see what she might have been up to in that very moment but was unable to act on such discernments due to Shadow's desire to stay rested until the merger was successfully completed. So, Ziva stayed put.

It was during this period of staying put, when Aries suddenly appeared before Ziva.

"There you are!" she exclaimed with eyes aglow. "I've found you."

Ziva already understood that although Aries grew increasingly powerful, she remained unaware of her true nature, while Ziva was unclear as to whether his sync-up with Shadow would be completed in time to destroy Aries.

"What place is this? What has happened to you, Ziva?" Aries asked. Upon receiving no response from Ziva, she continued. "Never mind, I'm certain all of the answers will soon come to me."

Ziva contended with Shadow. There was no time to stay put. If they didn't act now, they might be no match for Aries. It was also quite profound that she would even think to use Mystique as a radar for locating Ziva.

"Why so silent, Ziva? What are you up to?" She asked, her glowing eyes dancing. "You're not the same at all. Somehow, I can sense a different aura about you—within you. Why are you still alive?" She smiled wickedly. "Never mind that either. I will figure that part out, too. But while we wait, why don't I do this," Aries said, and began to chant:

> *"Spirits of the realm,*
> *force-field of all force-fields*
> *Return to Ziva's helm,*
> *Mystique, his bidden being.*
> *Protect my future dreams,*
> *From dream-spells that will harm me*
> *Return unto me my gift,*
> *So, the future I may again foresee."*

With that, Aries vanished. Ziva felt the need to quickly intercept whatever Aries had planned before she realized her true nature. But Ziva's thoughts suddenly gave way to Shadow's intentions of staying put.

Once again, Ziva contended with Shadow on a feasible strategy for safely delivering the people of Zannus Realm from Aries, and possibly retrieving the Nurians. They believed they would need to find a strategy that could be executed using a method that would block Aries from foreseeing the rescue. To top things off, such a feat would have to be achieved immediately, as Aries grew increasingly powerful with each passing moment. To make matters worse, Aries had located Ziva and could now discern him. Any moment now she would gain rapid awareness of Ziva's new form and location. There possibly would be no limit to her power of reach if shadow continued to dally.

Moments later, the synchronization of Shadow and Ziva was finalized. Ziva closed his eyes and engaged in deep meditation with Shadow.

CHAPTER 22
KINGDOM SVANIA

Back in Svania, Aries explored her growing powers. Her spur-of-the-moment decision to trap Mystique and use her to locate Ziva, and then getting rid of her, was quite impressive. She marveled at her ability to discern such extraordinary exploits and reveled in her genius. She wished for someone with whom to share her excitement but decided against the idea. She was now a force to be reckoned with.

Given that Ziva had used a dream spell to blind Aries in the past, Aries made sure that she beat Ziva at his own game. She had outsmarted Ziva by using his own trick against him. Firstly, she'd thrown Ziva's spell back at him by casting out Mystique. Secondly, she'd made sure that her spell included a dream protection mantra. Thirdly, she'd requested that the great force-field restore her gift of foresight, which was the only portion of the spell that remained unfulfilled. Aries had attempted taking down three beasts with one spell, so she suspended her desire for vengeance against her captors for better acclimation to her powers. Furthermore, they would clearly be no match for her. Acclimating to her powers could now be more easily achieved with Mystique out of her way.

Aries tried to summon her gift of foresight once again and was suddenly struck by a disturbing premonition. Standing in the shadows across the room was a half-naked woman with a dusty white sheet wrapped around her lower extremities. Her back was turned to Aries.

"Hello?" Aries called out to the woman, stunned at this vision's closeness to reality. The woman seemed so real that Aries felt the need to reach out and touch her.

"Hello," Aries called out again. The woman quickly turned to face Aries, whom, at the sight of her, gasped with perplexity. Aries realized that the woman was her own self.

"Ziva was here?" the woman asked.

"Me? Are you speaking to me?" Aries asked, confused.

"Yes, he was right here in this room, seducing you," a male voice said in the distance. The voice belonged to Akello. He sounded angry.

"Akello?" Aries whispered, quickly scanning the cell until her eyes rested upon Akello. He stood outside of the cell staring in at the woman in the vision—the woman who represented Aries.

"Aries? Are you in league with Ziva?" Akello asked.

"No, I'm not," the woman pleaded.

"Don't lie to me, Aries!"

"I'm not lying, Akello; you must believe me—I need your help."

"Senya was right about you," Akello fumed.

"You must believe me—you must listen to me ..."

"I'm done listening to you, Aries! I'm going to get my wizard, Qarhan. He will get to the bottom of this!" Akello stormed out, leaving the woman—Aries, alone.

The images slowly dissipated, leaving Aries to wrestle with the disturbing vision. She perceived in her vision feelings of aloneness, confusion, and devastation. She was angry about feeling this way. This vision was as frightful as it was illogical, but she knew there must be meaning to it. In her spell, she had asked for the ability to see the future once again. Was this it? Was her gift now returning to her in fragments? She was more confused now than she'd been before casting the spell. Aries discerned that her lack of clarity regarding her latest premonition was enough proof that her gift was far from being fully returned to her. This made her hesitant at completely embracing her growing powers without her full ability to foresee both near and far future. Acquisition of great powers, amidst the absence of her initial gift was almost intolerable.

As Aries grappled with fear of the unknown, Akello suddenly appeared before her.

"How long have you been standing there?" she asked, startled.

"Long enough to see that you are troubled," Akello replied pensively.

"Yet, if you knew what I know, it is you who would be troubled—not me," Aries hissed.

"Are you threatening your chief?" he asked.

"I'm merely educating you."

"I see no lessons in your threats. Nevertheless, I came by to offer you my sincerest apologies as well as a portion of my supper."

"You think I care for food and your miserable apology?"

"I didn't think you would care for either, though I hoped that you would."

"How is my pet?"

"I'm here to speak on that as well. I insisted that you be reunited with your cherolith. Senya has finally given in and offered to personally escort your pet to you at first light."

"So, you intend to keep me here overnight—against my will?"

"I feel responsible for your demise. You were going about your business, when I took your arm into mine, and literally whisked you away into ..."

"Imprisonment," Aries interjected.

"Yes, if it hadn't been for me, none of this would have happened to you."

"Then let me out of here!"

"I'm still working on that. Ziva has not yet returned, but I hope to arrive at a resolution with him as soon as he returns. Then you'll be free to go."

"How can you even be so sure of his return?" Aries asked, slightly shuddering at the reminder of Ziva. She hadn't really thought about him since their recent run-in. But now a series of questions flooded her thoughts. Questions such as how had he managed to survive? Why had he not yet come after her? Would she be ready if he did? What was the strange aura that she'd discerned about him? Where had he been hiding, and why?

"Did you hear my question?" Akello's voice disrupted her thoughts.

"Pardon me?" she said.

"I was asking you what you meant by your question. Should we not count on Ziva's return? Have you had a vision about him? Is he in trouble?"

"No," Senya said abruptly, recognizing the depth of her own deceit. She'd been furious about being manhandled and thrown into a dungeon for deceit. However, she could no longer stay angry at Akello, who had merely been a pawn in Senya's revenge tactic. Perhaps Aries would find it in her heart to forgive Akello. Afterall, had she been forthright, Senya would have had no useful ammunition against her. In fact, Aries intended to keep them all in the dark until she gained more clarity about her situation.

"I like you, Akello," she said softly.

"Do you now?" Akello gasped, quite taken aback.

"I do," she said inhaling deeply. "I'll consider accepting your apology."

"Why the change of heart?" he asked.

"No change of heart. I liked you the moment we met, and I still do."

"Then why lie to me about being blind?"

"I didn't lie to you. I was blind when we met. But by the time we arrived at the citadel, I'd regained my sight. Too frightened to share such an incredible tale, I kept up pretenses. The empress simply used the moment to get back at me for having the gift of foresight," Aries explained. Her senses were in overdrive. There was much to think about and very little time in which to do so.

"I need rest," she said, lying down on the cot.

"Then I will stay the night with you," Akello said, opening the gate and entering her cell. He seated himself next to the cot, his back against the wall. He watched in silence as Aries drifted off into peaceful slumber.

CHAPTER 23
Ziva: "To Parley or Not to Parley"

While Aries slept, she dreamed that she was sitting on the cot in the cell when Ziva appeared to her. He offered her a drink, and she accepted it gratefully because she was extremely thirsty. After an enormous swig from the cup, she asked:

"Why do you continue to haunt my dreams, Ziva?" Her thirst, now quenched, she took smaller sips from the cup and wondered what she was drinking. She also wondered how Ziva had acquired knowledge of her thirst in the first place. "Did my spell not work? Had I not commanded that you stay out of my dreams?"

"Your spell forbids me to harm you in your dreams, not to stay out of them," Ziva clarified.

"Let me guess; being the foolish and cowardly wizard that you are, you would rather connect with me through dreams, as opposed to real life, Isn't that right?" asked Aires, feeling euphoric.

"Dream-visits allow me easier access to your honesty," Ziva confessed.

"In other words, you're afraid that I might outwit you in real life," Aries retorted.

"I fear that you might use your gift of foresight to manipulate future outcomes."

"So, you admit to being a coward." Aries smiled coyly, feeling glorious.

"May I share with you why I'm here in your dreams?"

"You're asking permission this time," Aries sent Ziva a pensive gaze.

"I promise not to do anything you don't approve of," Ziva said.

"Is that so? Well, guess what? I already know that you can't do anything that I don't approve of, because I casted the protection spell. Remember?" Aries quipped.

"You're spell only prohibits me from harming you. It doesn't forbid me to do anything else."

"What else could there possibly be?" she asked feeling blissful. "What kind of drink is this? It's delicious."

"It's a potion of euphoria," Ziva answered forthrightly.

"A what?" she chuckled.

"A potion to make you feel good—so you don't view me as a threat," said Ziva, withholding the fact that the potion contained a spell to subdue Aries so he could easily extract her gift of foresight.

"Oh, you wish to trap me in my own dream."

"I wish to parley with you," he lied.

"Parley with me," Aries echoed drunkenly. "Tell you what—how about you and I exit this dream, and parley together in the real world?" she challenged, seemingly amused.

"I bade you not awake from this dream," Ziva quickly chanted.

"Wait, what?" Aries asked, perplexed. "You're forbidden to harm me in my dream, Ziva," she said, turning the cup to her head and downing the remainder of its contents.

"Try as I might, I'm unable to awake from this dream, Ziva. So, go ahead and begin your parley. Nothing you can do to harm me anyway." she advised.

"Thank you," Ziva said, marvelling at the brilliance his plan. He'd received the verbal agreement that he needed.

"I must confess my regrets of having wronged you in the past," he admitted, then paused to observe her reaction. Aries shrugged. She suddenly wondered whether her protection spell would release her from this dream should Ziva refuse to do so.

"But we are way beyond all of that now. Everything has changed--"

"Get to the point, Ziva," Aries interjected. "Why are you haunting my dreams? What is the reason for the potion of euphoria? Are you trying to seduce me? I thought you were a eunuch."

"I am no longer a eunuch, as you are no longer mortal." Ziva clarified. "But that is beside the point. I think you misunderstand me."

"You think that I'm immortal?" Aries chuckled. "Is that why you've lured me into this dream? Are you trying to seduce me because you think I'm now immortal?"

Ziva was aware that the effects of the potion would subside soon. He needed to work more quickly.

"I've been acquired by a new lifeforce, an entity that is much more powerful than I could ever imagine. We go on as Ziva, but my possessor's name is Shadow."

Ziva was aware that the effects of the potion would subside soon. He needed to work more quickly.

"I've been acquired by a new lifeforce, an entity that is much more powerful than I could ever imagine. We go on as Ziva, but my possessor's name is Shadow."

"Shadow!" Aries giggled. "A new lifeforce has possessed you so you're no longer a eunuch, and you decide to visit me in my dreams to possess me? Well, that's entertaining," she said, amused.

"I have grown far more powerful than anyone could ever imagine," Ziva continued.

"Hmm; I see," Aries said, pausing briefly before continuing, "I too have been growing inexplicably powerful." She announced this while smacking her lips loudly. "Was it my use of Mystique as a talisman to find you that caused you to believe that I'm immortal? I wouldn't blame you. I think that was my best trick yet."

"I am cognizant of your new powers, Aries; in fact, imagine how powerful we would be if we joined forces."

"Joined forces? How?" Aries asked.

"May I show you how?" Ziva asked.

"Sure, you may show me," Aries responded in amusement. She observed as Ziva kneeled before her, bringing his lips close to hers.

"You are seducing me," she uttered raspily against Ziva's lips. Feelings of Akello glided aside and into the distance, as the mighty wizard brushed lips with hers. Her loins quivered as Ziva softly asked again: "May I?"

"Yes," she whimpered, parting her lips.

Ziva linked his lips to hers and kissed her gently, at first, and then passionately. Satisfied at receiving the verbal permission he had needed, Ziva then murmured, "I breathe a part of my essence into you."

"And I, you," she replied, overcome by passion, and completely oblivious to Ziva's deceit.

"We are now bonded," Ziva said, slowly ending the kiss. "You, me, and Shadow are now bonded together. I've seized your gift of foresight. Going forward, we rule as a force to be reckoned with. However, you will answer only to me."

Aries had been rendered speechless. With the effects of the potion slowly dissipating, she gazed into Ziva's eyes, bewildered.

"Tonight's dream is now over," he whispered. "Wake up!" he said before vanishing.

Aries leaped up from her sleep, aghast.

"I'm up," she whispered breathlessly. However, Akello's terrified expression, along with the now beautifully lit room, warned Aries that more trouble was looming.

"I saw you," Akello said frantically.

"Pardon?"

"Your eyes—they're glowing; what—who are you?"

"Yes—I can explain ..."

"Get dressed," Akello ordered pacing anxiously about the cell.

"Wait! Why am I naked?" Aries asked, frantically scanning the room for the answer. She grabbed the dusty white sheet and wrapped it around her lower extremities.

"I have just witnessed Ziva seduce you, undress you, and kiss you. All of this he did right in front of me."

"Wait, you could see him?"

"Yes, I called after him— but he remained fixated on you, and then he left the room!"

"It wasn't really—It couldn't be real," she stuttered.

"But it was real, and Ziva was here," Akello confirmed.

"Why didn't you call for me—wake me up? He appeared to me in my dream. You should have called out to me ..."

"I did, but to no avail. What's going on Aries? Are you in league with Ziva?"

"No, I'm not!"

"Don't lie to me, Aries!"

"I'm not lying, Akello. You must believe me—I need your help. In my dream—Ziva informed me that he's been possessed by a powerful entity—Shadow. They've joined forces!"

"Senya was right about you-"

"Akello, you must listen to me ..."

"I'm done listening to you, Aries! I'm going to get Wizard Qarhan. He will get to the bottom of this!" Akello stormed off leaving Aries feeling alone, distraught and confused. The incident had transpired, just as she'd foreseen it. She wished she could foresee what would happen next. How had Ziva managed to trick her—again? Aries was suddenly overcome with a feeling of dread as she perceived Ziva—and the unknown entity within him, seizing her cherolith from its hidden confinement right before vanishing with it. She was then struck with a premonition of the Nurian's escape from Zannus Realm. She experienced sudden compulsion to go after them. Retrieve them. Aware of her power spurt, she allowed a flood of visions to overcome her. She could now perceive the goings-on within other kingdoms, and even territories beyond Zannus Realm. Aries deduced that her gift had only just now fully returned to her, though not in the way she had expected. Nevertheless, she welcomed the return of her gift of foresight, satisfied at the vast powers she now possessed. Given that her gift of foresight had only just now fully returned to her, it meant that Ziva had not been successful in acquiring her gift of foresight after all.

CHAPTER 24
Aries: "I am Magnificent"

Aries fell to her knees and whipped her head up towards the skies yelling:

"Terrlashnavek Kabet Lavimiyk, Ziva!" Lightning flashed and thunder roared as the earth shook. The walls of the dungeon gave way as it collapsed upon itself.

Boulders and rubbles amassed about Aries, but none of it touched her. "Terrlashnavek Kabet Lavimiyk, Ziva!" she repeated feverishly. She clasped her hands and intoned:

> *"Oh, great force-field of force-fields!*
> *Bade me the light of Zannus!*
> *Withdraw from me these essences--*
> *Imposed upon my subconscious.*
> *Undo kin synapses,*
> *And unlink every axon,*
> *Bring forth both partial entities,*
> *To serve me as my weapon!"*

With eyes still aglow, Aries watched as two ghost-like figures withdrew from her. One of them represented a partial essence of Shadow, and the other represented a partial essence of Ziva. Both representing the two portions of essences gifted by Ziva to Aries earlier in her dream, when Ziva breathed his essence into her, thus fashioning a bond between himself, Aries and Shadow. As she acclimatized to her new self, Aries was ready to fully accept that she was seamlessly magnificent and powerful.

This feat was as terrifying for her as it was splendid. Drained, Aries sauntered through the rubble and sat on a massive boulder. She perceived that Akello would soon return with the others, but she had greater priorities at hand.

"You are truly powerful," remarked the Shadow essence. "You have successfully ripped us away from our masters, and now we belong to you. When you have destroyed Ziva and Shadow, we will remain with you, as you have untethered us from both beings."

"I will use you to destroy your roots, Shadow and Ziva. You may return to me, but only as I command. Selavimiyk sperrosehes. Terrlashnavek Kabet miyk. I bid you enter me as my subjects." Aries closed her eyes as the essences wafted back into her body. She revisited her discernment of the Nurians. She perceived that something had gone awry with them. They were trapped on a strange planet, and their intended destination was planet earth. The immediate perception continued to unravel as Aries made her way to the location of the Nurians.

"Dijimonek olosek, America, seet planet earth!" she yelled, as an illuminated energy cloud engulfed her just as Akello returned with his crew. They watched dumbfounded as Aries was swept up and away by the energy cloud.

CHAPTER 25
Wizard Qarhan: "Tongue of the LifeForce"

The events that occurred after Akello stormed out of Aries cell in the dungeon are as follows:

Immediately following their fight in the dungeon, Akello had stormed away from Aries, intent on retrieving Wizard Qarhan, Empress Senya, and his men, to aid in properly interrogating Aries. He needed reinforcements in efforts of successfully thrashing both Ziva and Aries. But what Akello didn't know was that his wizard had been present, in spirit, with both him and Aries the whole time, witnessing Ziva seduce Aries. Yes, Wizard Qarhan had once again ventured outside of his own body and into the dungeon, tailing Akello. In fact, Wizard Qarhan had immediately perceived a foreign aura as soon as Ziva sneaked into the dungeon. Ziva had made himself invisible while he attentively listened in on the entire conversation between Aries and Akello. Qarhan, who was also invisible, had perceived Ziva's presence, moments before he actually appeared to Akello. Qarhan had even struggled with thoughts of whether Ziva would perceive him. However, from the looks of things, it was clear that Ziva had no knowledge of Qarhan's unique presence in the dungeon. Neither had Ziva acknowledged Akello who was sitting next to Aries while she slept on the cot. What Qarhan found the strangest, was that Ziva, having heard Akello and Aries all but confess their love for one another, had still proceeded with seducing Aries anyway. Throughout this episode, he had even ignored Akello's shouts for him to stop, and after the seduction, had left the cell, unaware of being tailed—by Wizard Qarhan's spirit.

During his exit, Ziva had stopped at the cell where the hideous cherolith was being held. The animal growled ferociously but Ziva whispered: "Selavimiyk, cherolith," and the beast immediately calmed.

Qarhan's shock at these words almost sent him spiraling back into his room where he had left his physical body, because he'd recognized the word *Selavimiyk*, which was the secret tongue of the ancient archetypal lifeforces. He'd recalled the language from many centuries ago, when it was used to breathe the essence of enchantment into him. *Selavimiyk* meant *"you now serve me,"* which was what Qarhan had whispered to the beast.

The cell door unlocked at these words and the beast ambled through it into Ziva's arms.

"Dijimonek olosek," Ziva whispered, before vanishing with the cherolith.

Wizard Qarhan decided he'd already discovered too much. *Had Ziva been acquired by a lifeforce?* Qarhan suddenly felt himself being forcefully pulled away from the dungeon, back towards the citadel—in the room where his body was. He dived back into his body just in time to hear the worrisome chatter of the group that had gathered by his bedside.

"I swear to you that Ziva and Aries are behind this. First, I had to watch Ziva seduce Aries in her sleep. Now they're both attacking Asteria's wizard. Qarhan, wake up!" Akello shouted, rigorously shaking Wizard Qarhan.

Qarhan slowly opened his eyes and cautiously arose from the bed. He woozily eyed his anxious audience.

"Finally! Thank the moons, he's alive!" councilman two exclaimed with a sigh of relief.

"Qarhan, are you ok?" asked Empress Senya.

"I'm well," Qarhan said groggily.

"We've been shouting your name for quite some time now," the councilmen chorused.

"And I've been shaking you like a mad man!" Akello exclaimed pensively. "I feel as if I've lost my wits because I just encountered a distressing incident—I witnessed Ziva seducing Aries in the dungeon!" Akello said urgently.

"Wait, what?" Senya squirmed.

"Qarhan, I'm glad that you're back with us. if you are well, then I need you—I need you all to accompany me back to the dungeon, at once!"

"I'm ok—actually I was just having a vision about an incident in the dungeon," Qarhan replied coyly. He was not ready to announce his gift of astral projection—his ability to leave his body. Instead, he lied that he had a vision. This would greatly simplify things.

"You had a vision?" Senya's maidens chorused as they entered the room. The group turned instantly to look at them.

"Ladies, I gave you the night off," Senya said to them.

"Yes, Empress, but we were across the way when we heard you hollering for Qarhan to wake up. We came to see if all is well with our guest."

"All is well ladies and thank you all for your concern" Qarhan said, slowly rising from the bed.

"Since when were you able to foresee things to come?" Akello asked curiously.

"This was my first time," Qarhan replied. "As I was explaining," he continued, "I had a vision of Ziva."

"I didn't know that you could have visions," Akello chimed in.

"If you haven't noticed, Akello, things are changing very fast within our realm," Qarhan replied.

"Indeed," Akello agreed, satisfied with this response, as it perfectly matched his own sentiments of recent events.

"Is Wizard Ziva in trouble?" Senya asked cautiously. Knowingly.

"Yes. I think that Ziva is in a heap of trouble," Qarhan confirmed. The small gathering gasped fearfully. Akello listened attentively.

"What's wrong with Ziva?" councilman six asked.

"Ziva may no longer be Ziva, and your kingdom—all of Zannus realm may be at risk," said Qarhan.

"Tell us about your vision" urged Akello.

"I think that something—a dangerous entity has completely taken over the Ziva that we once knew."

"Taken over? How? Isn't that impossible?" asked councilman five.

"Not impossible," Senya chimed in. "I assumed the worse when the waters of our fountain of youth suddenly turned murky before vanishing."

"You didn't think to share this bit of information with us prior to now?" Akello asked sternly.

"I planned on sharing this news with you at first light. I was hoping that Wizard Ziva would finally arrive tonight and fix everything," she lied. "Tell us, Qarhan—is Ziva coming back to us?"

This question caught Qarhan off guard, as he had no idea of Ziva's plans or whereabouts. He glanced around at the group, deftly averting Akello's piercing gaze.

"Ziva is now possessed by an evil entity. This evil entity has also seized the cherolith from its cage," he said.

"So, is Ziva still here—is he coming back? Is he in league with Aries?" Senya asked, stunned.

"I—in—my vision, I saw Ziva vanishing with the beast, right after seducing Aries in front of you, Akello," replied Qarhan.

Akello nodded vigorously, "Yes—I believe you. Your vision must be right because Ziva did seduce Aries right in front of me."

"But isn't he a eunuch?" Senya asked curiously, remembering a previous conversation she'd had with Aries on the same topic.

"Your vision is accurate," Akello reiterated, ignoring Senya's question. "Ziva did seduce Aries right before my eyes—I yelled—and screamed—I hollered for him to stop—to explain himself—but he just carried on without the slightest acknowledgment of my presence there right next to him!"

"Ziva? Seducing Aries?" exclaimed a bewildered Senya. She wondered how any of this could ever be true. How long had she tried to seduce Ziva to no avail? For years Senya had attributed Ziva's rebuff of her advances to the fact that he was a eunuch. How had Aries gotten Ziva to seduce her, when Senya had been the one seeking to seduce Ziva in the first place?

When Senya had discovered that Aries wasn't actually blind; she'd concluded that Aries had once again tricked her. Ziva's disappearance along with Senya's inability to put the pieces together, had led her to spontaneous action when the opportunity presented itself for her to lock Aries away in the dungeon. However, the news about Ziva's re-appearance in the dungeon, and his seduction of Aries, completely mortified her. Senya had no doubt that the lifeforce was dead. Which meant that Ziva should have been dead with it. How could another entity have possessed him? Unless Aries had lied about Ziva's connection to the water-force. Not that she'd wanted the water-force or Ziva dead, but shouldn't Ziva have been destroyed along with the water-force? What had Aries not lied about? Yet, if Aries had been lying all along, where had Ziva been all this time? What were his motives? Given Senya's closeness to Ziva, and the fact that she was chosen by the lifeforce to be empress, shouldn't she have been the object of Ziva's affection, instead of duplicitous Aries? There was nothing she could do now as it seemed Aries had somehow coaxed her way to victory.

"Did you all hear that?" Qarhan said, disrupting Senya from her thoughts. Thunder roared out in the night sky, as the ground beneath them shook. They clutched each other's arms for support, to keep from tumbling over. Containers and uplighters crashed to the floor as tables toppled. The rumbling and commotion were brief but left the group gasping in horror.

"Sounded as if that came from the dungeon," said Qarhan.

"Agreed," the guards chorused.

"We should head over there immediately!" yelled Akello.

The small gathering made their way to the dungeon, in efforts of locating the source of the commotion. The sight that greeted them was enigmatic. The entrance to the dungeon was blocked by wreckage from the quake.

"What's the meaning of this?" Senya asked Akello.

"Qarhan, help us get through the rubble," Akello said to Qarhan.

Without hesitation, Qarhan murmured a chant as he pointed his staff towards the wreckage. The sound of rumbling returned but much softer than before. Boulders and debris immediately hoisted themselves out the way, thus clearing the path for the anxious group to resume their hurried journey to Aries' cell. "Follow me," Qarhan said, "just a minor detour this way."

"But Aries' cell is not in that direction—it' straight ahead," Serena rebuffed. She was anxious to find out what had taken place with Aries.

"I understand—but at the very least we should check to see if the cherolith is still where we had left it," Qarhan explained.

"He's right," Akello agreed, "if the cherolith is gone, then that would further confirm Qarhan's vision."

"Agreed," said Senya, her heart somersaulting inside her.

They all made the detour with Qarhan, and to his satisfaction, the cell in which the cherolith was placed was empty and unaffected by the quake. The beast was gone. But of course, Wizard Qarhan already knew that.

"It's just as Qarhan's vision had predicted," Serena exclaimed. They all nodded in agreement. However, Ziva was unclear about the eventual outcome of his lie. He hoped that Leo's words to Akello would come to pass, that Qarhan just might assume the powers of Svania's lifeforce, in Ziva's absence. Qarhan wondered whether Ziva's transformation or his own lie about having a vision would get him any closer to assuming the power of Svania's lifeforce. He was stirred from his thoughts when Akello exclaimed, "We need to see about Aries!" The group immediately turned and scurried towards Aries' cell. As they drew closer, a bright light illuminated about them. They looked ahead in the direction of the source to see a bright cloud of energy engulf Aries before heaving her above ground level.

"Dijimonek olosek, United States of America, seet planet earth!" Aries shouted, as the bright cloud of energy lifted her through the opening in the roof which had collapsed during the mysterious quake. Aries glanced down at her spectators who watched in bewilderment as the energy cloud carted her away.

CHAPTER 26
The Nurians: Presently

The Nurians had fled their kingdom using the portal that Emperor Lunar and his team created. The procedure for their escape involved boarding a spacecraft, which was then propelled through the portal, which should have transported them to a river gorge on earth but did not. Destination Oregon, Planet Earth, was deemed by intelligence officers as ideal for undetected landings. The spacecraft that now hosted the Nurians was once kept hidden from the Asterian government through the use of Nuria's covert technology invisibility cloak. This method of concealment was as ingenious as the creation of a portal for space travel.

It's a wonder that the Nurians found themselves displaced and their space vessel floating above the surface of what appeared to be a red planet. Although they were ejected from the portal, their spaceship did not land, because a force, unfamiliar to them, prevented them from landing. Intelligence officers worked as quickly as possible to gather all they could about their newfound dilemma. Emperor Lunar surmised that the spacecraft remained floating, and they remained floating in it, because of the red planet's zero-mass attraction. This was a term Nurians used to describe the absence of what people of earth referred to as gravity, which kept everything from falling off the planet.

The intelligence officers found it difficult to maneuver the spacecraft due to the zero-mass attraction which continuously forced them to float above the cockpit of their air vessel, while the air vessel floated above the red planet's surface. Chaos erupted outside of the cockpit area, as the Nurians struggled to understand this unexpected and seemingly inexplicable situation. Everyone was terrified of not having reached their intended destination, and even more terrified that the space vessel had suddenly began to lose oxygen, thus making breathing difficult.

"We're almost out of oxygen," Taurus wheezed. He clutched a rail to keep from floating off. He gasped for air and his colleagues followed suit.

"I can hardly breathe—I need to see about my wife," Lunar wheezed, grabbing his throat.

"It's hard to navigate zero mass attraction while struggling for air," Caleb panted.

"I'm guessing that this is the atmosphere of a planet with little to no oxygen," Lunar said eyeing the partial pressure detection warning signal.

"Our sensors have detected very little wormhole matter," Atlas shared, gasping for air.

"Does this mean that our portal is almost dried up?" Sirius panted, terrified.

"Yes—isn't this the same thing that happened to Wizard Ziva? When he ventured into our kingdom—the portal had spat him out mid-air!" Caleb rasped.

"It's not the same," Taurus countered, his voice almost a croak. "Our failure to land is due to zero mass attraction, not a faulty magical portal."

"But we are here because of a faulty magical portal, are we not?" panted Sirius.

"No, we are not!" Taurus croaked, grabbing his chest.

"This is very wrong—we promised our people earth, and this is clearly not it," gasped Caleb, who was now struggling to wrap his thoughts around the significant drop in temperature.

"It's freezing all of a sudden," Lunar admitted, shivering.

"The temperature meter indicates absolute freezing point—the gauge has settled on the sub-cooling point."

"What?" the group chorused in shock. Sirius and Skylar erupted into bouts of coughing, a result of the high carbon dioxide content of the red planet's atmosphere.

"Any moment now we'll either freeze to death, or die from lack of oxygen," Taurus panted.

"Amira," Lunar wheezed. He hoisted himself toward the doors of the cockpit, in efforts of recovering his wife. But it was too late. Lunar's body gave way, and he fainted.

Just before the others also fainted, there was a loud commotion of hundreds of Nurians crying out for oxygen outside of the cockpit. There was nothing that any ordinary person could do to help them. Their extraordinary intellect seemed to have ultimately costed them their lives.

Chapter 27

The cloud of energy which had transported Aries out of the
dungeon and away from Akello and his flunkies, changed course
immediately after departing Zannus realm. Aries, suddenly
cognizant of the Nurian's displacement on the red planet,
summoned a wormhole through which she guided her energy
cloud. She was delighted that her powers were rapidly developing,
and even more ecstatic for being able to do anything she willed her
mind to. She wondered whether she would become an all-seeing
being. She smiled at that idea. Would her gift of foresight grow to
such magnitudes?

Aries recalled her seamless detour after leaving Zannus Realm. She
remembered shouting out her destination to earth, while being
carted away by her energy cloud. This was an enchantment
method she had immediately regretted as she was certain that
Akello and all of the realm's forces may have heard her. She was
therefore thankful that the Nurians did not arrive on planet earth,
as this might have worked out for the best, in case any Zannusian,
or any lifeforce, entertained thoughts of tracking all of them to
earth. Her vision of the Nurians had grown cleared when she made
the detour and headed to the red planet.

Moments later the energy cloud resurfaced from the portal into
which it had vanished. Aries arrived at the red planet afloat her
energy cloud. At Aries' bidding, an oxygenated bubble filled with
warmth was generated by the energy cloud, which formed a
protective shield that enveloped Aries and the massive floating

spacecraft that contained hundreds of oxygen deprived Nurians that were knocking at death's door. Aries perceived glimmers of life within the ship, an indication that the Nurians still lived, but ventured at the cusp of death. The oxygen bubble would hopefully revive them soon.

Without entering the ship, Aries closed her eyes, inhaled deeply, and summoned Emperor Lunar's spirit before it had a chance to return to its reviving host.

"Where am I?" Lunar asked upon arrival before Aries.

"You and your people remain displaced, but I'm giving you the chance to save everyone—including yourself, Lunar" Aries said, pensively.

"A chance to save everyone? But haven't we all died? In fact, who are you? How am I here—before you?"

"Hmm, I suppose you could consider me extraordinary. I am a powerful force, and I'm here to save you and your people."

"Extraordinary? A powerful force?"

"Yes, I have casted a protective shield filled with oxygen and warmth, over your transport vessel. Although this will not last for long, what other than an extraordinarily powerful force could do such a thing?"

"Uh—I guess you're right, so long as this is all real and I'm not hallucinating," Lunar shrugged.

"Enough of that, Lunar, you need to trust me—this is all real. My powers are still emerging, but this red planet is already draining me of them."

"I must be crossing over..."

"You are not dying," Aries said, quickly cutting him off, "your people are recouping as we speak. You'll be the last one to recover, as I have summoned you here with me. But if things do not go as I hope, I'll be forced to retrieve my oxygen shield, before leaving you all here."

"We would simply suffer all over again…"

"But you have the chance to prevent that from happening."

"Let's say you speak the truth, and I am not hallucinating, what exactly do you want from me in return for saving us all?"

"Very well. I'm about to tell you something, but once I do, you'll have a decision to make. I must warn you though, we don't have much time, so you must make your decision quickly, because not only do my powers dwindle on this red planet, I'm also now perceiving a dangerous summoning back at Zannus Realm. I must quickly return to Zannus for a great battle. Do you understand this?"

"So, you are here from Zannus—how did you find us? Has Qarhan been tracking us? Did he send you here for us?"

"Yes, I'm from Zannus, and no—this has nothing to do with Wizard Qarhan …."

"But how do you know my name?"

"As you can see, I'm rather powerful, and I perceive many things about many people. I need to know that you understand that the lives of your people depend on your quick decision, because any moment now I must leave you."

"Ok, I'm open to hearing you out."

"Good," Aries inhaled with relief. "I belong to Kingdom Svania."

"Svania?"

"Yes. In summary, a not-so-innocent curiosity of mine, led me down an enchanted path that has now triggered powers I didn't know existed within me. Prior to all of this, I was just an ordinary seer…"

"A seer?"

"Yes, before all of this, my people sought after me for my ability to foresee things."

"You can see the future?"

"Yes, I'm glad you're catching on quickly. Amidst my power spurt, the Svanian lifeforce collapsed, thus awakening a more powerful and dangerous lifeforce that seeks absolute control of all of Zannus Realm."

"What?"

"Yes—as we speak, this evil force…"

""Well—at this moment, he is neither dead nor alive. The new lifeforce—Shadow he calls himself—has possessed Ziva. Shadow has now stricken Ziva's essence and is now summoning Wizard Qarhan for reasons I presume are dangerous to all of the realm. Anyway, I can get you out of here, but only if you agree to return to Nuria, your Kingdom."

"We couldn't! The Asterians…"

"Forget about the Asterians. You know, I could protect you and your people from the Asterians. So, you can either trust me and get out of here or stay here and die."

"So, you'll save us from this red planet, as well as the Asterians, but you haven't said what's in it for you."

"Very well. As you can see, I'm powerful enough to stand against Shadow, the Asterians, and Wizard Qarhan—but win or lose, I'll be completely shattered after today's upcoming events," Aries paused briefly, then continued be completely shattered after today's upcoming events," Aries paused briefly, then continued. "Whether or not I lose, I need to borrow the essences of two hundred and fifty of your men."

"Borrow the essences? Meaning what exactly?"

"It simply means I get to borrow their lives, just for this battle. My powers grow stronger but saving you has severely weakened me. Plus, I highly doubt that I have sufficient wisdom to beat an ancient lifeforce such as Shadow, so I'll need all the strength that I can get. Borrowing the essences of these men should give me a fighting chance."

"Wait—you wish to take the lives of nearly one third of my kingdom?"

"It's no longer your kingdom, and their lives would be returned to them."

"But—you're no different from this Shadow if your intent is for me to sacrifice the lives of my people."

"Looks like you've already sacrificed their lives by removing them from Nuria. Don't forget that you're the reason why they're in this predicament. My time has almost run out. As sworn emperor and leader of your people, I need your spoken approval to enter a covenant on behalf of the Nurian kingdom, authorizing me to temporarily extract the essences of two hundred and fifty Nurian men, who will have their essences returned to them at the end of today's battle with Shadow."

"Why didn't you ask this of your own Svanian people?" Lunar asked rebelliously.

"Because they're all women," Aries replied bluntly. "I need the essences of men. Your spoken word, Lunar; are you ready for the swearing in? Quickly, we are nearly out of time. I must return to fight."

"As seer, can you guarantee the safe return of the essences of my men?"

"I have not yet seen the outcome of this battle, and this planet has been draining my abilities. But rest assured, I have a trick up my sleeve that Shadow won't see coming. I may not even have to risk the lives of your men. But I need your spoken spoke approval, Lunar. Now."

"Ok, ok—I'm ready."

"Good, because your people have awoken inside the aircraft, and are busy trying to shake you back to life. Your wife is already mourning your death, and everyone is confused," Aries offered a subtle smile.

"What do I need to say?"

"Very well, repeat after me. Lifeforce of all lifeforces ..."

Emperor Lunar did as he was directed by the now powerful Aries, echoing after her, words spoken in a language unknown to him, tying two hundred and fifty of his men to Aries.

Upon conclusion of the enchantment, Lunar was released back into his body, and into the embrace of his wife and comrades. The people's loud cheering suddenly quieted seemingly as quickly as it had begun. The Nurians watched in shock as numerous men suddenly lost consciousness and floated about the aircraft.

Meanwhile, outside, the oxygen bubble that engulfed Aries, her energy cloud, and the Nurians' aircraft, were guided into the portal that Aries had arrived in. The oxygen bubble quickly vanished from the red planet, reappearing in Nuria almost immediately afterwards.

Inside the aircraft, Lunar braced himself for facing his bewildered followers. He briefly considered sharing the truth with them but opted to pretend as if he too was bewildered and confused about what had just transpired. He managed to buy himself enough time to cook up a plausible lie.

CHAPTER 28
Shadow

The spell that Aries had casted when she'd seized Ziva and Shadow's essences, had been so masterfully executed that Ziva and Shadow remained temporarily frozen as they watched the events unfold through the glow of Shadow's rudenium stone. The ritual had almost completely immobilized them. The partial forfeiture of both Shadow and Ziva's essences resulted in a flow of power from both beings into the portion of their essences that were now tethered to Aries. Aries' unanticipated ploy now left Shadow and Ziva befuddled and weak, even after the ritual had ended. As they regained composure, Ziva and Shadow contended between themselves as to whose fault it was that caused this.

Shadow was never more livid, and contended that Ziva's seduction of Aries should have never transpired in the first place, as this was against Shadow's own will, and was never a part of their mutual plan for subduing Aries. Shadow reminded Ziva that the original agreement was to visit Aries while she slept and trap her in her dream, leaving her trapped there—for eternity. It was a perfect plan that was simple enough and bound to work, as trapping Aries in a pleasant dream would not technically count as harming her, and thus would not have been hindered by her previous dream protection spell. The idea was at the very least, worth a try. Yet, Ziva had resisted this plan and suppressed Shadow within him, to carry out his own seduction plan. Shadow had remained in suppression, to observe Ziva's movements, while hoping that Ziva would redeem himself—however, when it appeared that Ziva had zero intentions of reconciling his error, Shadow finally fought to gain control. It was too late. Ziva had successfully stifled Shadow's being, at least temporarily.

Shadow further contended that Ziva had only worsened matters by allowing himself to be seen performing the seduction and ignoring Akello in the process. Against their mutual plan, Ziva had returned to Kingdom Svania, visiting the Pterion Springs where the water-force once dwelled. It was Ziva whom had concocted the plan to visit and seduce Aries in her dream.

"You were so busy focusing on keeping me suppressed that you completely missed Akello's presence in the dungeon as well as his screams for you to comport yourself," Shadow scowled.

Aghast at Shadow's perspective, Ziva attempted to murmur something under his breath. "I—I ..."

"Enough Ziva!" Shadow said cutting him off. "At first, I remained suppressed hoping you would come to your senses. But then I tried to stop you and it was too late. You accessed my powers and used them against me. If you hadn't blocked my attempts at stopping you, we wouldn't have to now shoulder the potential disadvantage you have caused us. You have weakened us through your selfish actions, seducing Aries, and stealing her gift of foresight as well as her pet cherolith." Shadow briefly scanned the area as if attempting to locate the newly acquired beast that Ziva had brought back with him to Octushi. "Come to think of it, why have we not yet been granted visions of things to come? Why can we not foresee the future? Where is the gift that you've supposedly confiscated from Aries?"

"It's possible that we might still be acclimating to it," Ziva tried his best to sound sure of himself.

Shadow brought forth his rudenium stone once again and murmured something beneath his breath as he glided a palm over the stone. The stone immediately came alive with glowing images of what Ziva recognized as the dungeon in which he'd seduced Aries in her dream. He and Shadow watched in silence as an energy cloud engulfed Aries and carted her away from a small, bewildered group. "Dijimonek olosek, United States of America, seet planet earth!" Aries had said before vanishing.

"It appears our nemesis is headed to planet earth. We have no clue of her motives. The loss of our essences has weakened us too much for us to even attempt to track her or anyone else outside of Zannus Realm, let alone follow and retrieve them from another planet. The powers of my rudenium stone have shifted. How can we possibly prevent our realm's collapse in this weakened state?" Shadow contended angrily.

"I—I'm so sorry—this situation is both new and difficult for me. Let us try again, Shadow. Let's grant ourselves another opportunity to work together and aim to find a mutual solution," Ziva begged.

"This situation may be new to me, but it's not new to you, Ziva. You refuse to learn your lesson. It was these very actions of yours that cost you your kingdom and lifeforce. I should have trusted my better instincts to let you pass on, instead of further risking the continuity of Zannus realm by teaming up with you. How could I have trusted a being that worked against his own water-force?"

"Shadow, please grant me one last chance. I can't even believe I've brought desolation to our realm because of my own selfishness," pled Ziva.

"It's far too late now," Shadow spat. "You've already ruined so much. Your actions have weakened us and cost us enough. This path was never what I envisioned for our union." Without missing a beat, Shadow spoke aloud: "By the powers granted unto us through the ancient archetypal lifeforces, I hereby surrender my gift of wielding the powers of the rudenium stone, in exchange for the power to relegate my host to the background of our being. I bid you collapse, Ziva, so that my essence alone will break through!" Immediately, Ziva felt himself overcome by this simple but powerful command as he became trapped in the background of himself, while Shadow's essence broke through as the dominant being. It was never Shadow's intention to surrender his power of wielding the rudenium stone. It wasn't his intention of surrendering any power at all in exchange for complete dominion over Ziva's body. His intention was to honor the grounds of their union. However, Ziva had audaciously broken their agreement, consequently putting Shadow at a severe disadvantage. Ziva had once again proven himself untrustworthy. Shadow needed him out of the way immediately. Shadow, now severely weakened by the actions of Ziva, as well as his recent surrender of his powers, would no longer be able to use the rudenium stone to see things that were occurring in places where he was not present. This was a huge disadvantage as his rival, Aries, would now have competitive edge over him. Shadow grew increasingly concerned about this. Certainly, he'd been around for much longer than Aries, and his wisdom was vast. He would have to try to draw strength from such, to bring Aries to her knees, and recover from her the parts of himself that she now possessed. Additionally, Shadow remained hopeful at his prospect of acclimating to the gift of foresight that Ziva had seized from Aries. He would use this gift to his advantage as soon as it became active within him. As a matter of fact, Shadow briefly wondered why this gift of foresight that Ziva had confiscated had not yet arrived.

The cherolith wandered into his line of sight and an idea suddenly dawned on Shadow.

"Terrlashnavek Kabet suspehes ay miyk, mustrak!" Shadow recited, commanding the beast to speak.

"Oslavo, terrselavu," the beast replied in obedience, its voice booming and frightful.

"Oslavo, terrselavu," the beast repeated, his response meaning: *Master, I serve you.*

"Indeed," Shadow said gleefully, "Wizard Ziva might have been on to something," he smiled wickedly. "Aries took something of ours, and we've reciprocated the favor."

"How might I be of service to you, master?" the beast boomed terrifyingly.

"Well," Shadow said pensively, "there must be something you know about Aries—a weakness, or weaknesses that you can share with me. Give me something that I can use against her," Shadow reasoned with the cherolith. Shadow purposefully withheld his potential plan to coax Aries into a barter, which would involve Aries returning his essences to him, in exchange for her cherolith. Recovery of the Ziva and Shadow essences would mean gradual recovery of Shadow's ability to wield the powers of his rudenium stone again.

"Master, I possibly do have some knowledge that might be of some use to you," offered the cherolith.

"Hmm," Shadow grunted raising a curious brow.

"Aries has lost her gift of foresight," shared the beast.

"Wrong!" replied Shadow, "I know for a fact that Aries has this gift."

"She had the gift," the beast corrected, "as I've said, she's lost it. I alone was present during those times when she fussed at her failed attempts at reigniting this gift she recently lost." The beast paused briefly to allow his bewildered master a moment of composure, then he continued. "I suppose you may also need to know that someone else was in the dungeon with us when you seized me from my cell," said the beast.

"Of course, I'm aware that Aries and Akello were both in the dungeon at the time. There couldn't have been anyone else." Shadow's thoughts lingered on the shocking news about Aries losing her gift of foresight.

"That's where you're wrong, master. As a cherolith, I possess a special kind of power for sensing things—even seeing things that you cannot see, great master."

"Mind your tongue, beast," Shadow grimaced. He contemplated whether the beast was lying to him. But he knew that the servitude spell he'd performed in subduing the cherolith would have rendered lying impossible.

"Sorry master," the beast continued, "but what I say is true."

"Explain yourself," Shadow commanded. The news about Aries' gift, or loss thereof, would only adversely impact Shadow if Aries had lost this gift before Wizard Ziva had performed his spell to seize it. Such a situation would trigger what's known by lifeforces to be a 'null'. A null was referred to as a rare occurrence that was triggered in the event of a spell being cast for nothing, like in Ziva's case. The powers within the spell were dispensed, but ultimately wasted, so an occurrence or a null was incurred. Two or more nulls would possibly result in the Double Null Enchantment which could ultimately be used in the dissolution of the lifeforce that incurred them.

"Master, someone other than Akello and Aries was present in the dungeon with us—in spirit. And this someone had been watching every move you made," the cherolith snarled.

"You mean: Astral projection?" Shadow asked pensively, bending down to level with the beast. "Whom?" he asked calmly, but inwardly battling a flood of intrusive thoughts.

"The Wizard of Asteria," the beast replied.

"Qarhan? Are you sure of this?"

"Of course, I'm sure. It was him and his master, Chief Akello, and others who had us thrown into the dungeon. I'm sure it was Qarhan's presence that I had seen."

"Hmm," Shadow said raising a thoughtful brow once more, and very much aware of his new ability to do so. "Was Akello aware of this?"

"It didn't appear so, master."

"Am I to understand that Wizard Qarhan secretly engages in astral travel?"

"I could clearly see him—his spirit, following us—even though he's not dead." the beast growled.

"Hmm," Shadow repeated, his thoughts consuming him. Shadow stood and began pacing in silence. Meanwhile the beast surmised that Shadow must have been bothered by his lack of astral projection powers.

Moments later Shadow yelled, "he too must serve me!"

"Who?" asked the beast.

"Wizard Qarhan of course! I will make him my loyal subject, but not before confiscating his secret gift of astral projection. I have a solid plan to destroy Aries and reclaim my essences. Everyone throughout this realm will be given no choice but to bow down to me. I will make

Aries pay for what she has done. When did Aries lose her gift?" Shadow finally asked the beast.

"She's been secretly fussing about this since before we got thrown into the dungeon," replied the beast confirming Shadow's worst fear.

Shadow was now perturbed more than ever by what he considered to be foolish acts of Ziva. He had fortunately gained a physical body, but unfortunately lost immeasurable powers in the process. To make matters worse, thanks to Ziva, he had inadvertently acquired powers that were null, when Ziva had bonded essences with Aries to subdue her and seize her gift of foresight, a gift, which, according to the cherolith, Aries did not possess at the time. If this was the case, and Shadow was almost certain that this was the case, he'd now found himself in a predicament. The 'Double Null Enchantment' could be used against him if he did not carefully strategize. The enchantment of Double Null was an ancient charm used by powerful beings to thwart possible greed. In other words, lifeforces, and powerful other-worldly beings, were allowed two chances, throughout the duration of their existence, to attempt to seize another's power and fail. Each failure was considered a null, and each null reduced the power of the robber. Accumulation of two or more nulls would be grounds for enforcing the Double Null Enchantment, which could be used by these powerful entities, as they deemed fit. But there was a catch. The performer of the charm must have specific knowledge of each null, and during the enchantment state a minimum of two nulls accrued by the accused. The enchantment was highly dangerous as it could potentially end the existence of an entity, or backfire on the enchanter if any of the nulls were incorrectly stated.

Shadow carefully contemplated the gravity of the situation. While he recovered from the tiff he had with Ziva before repressing the wizard, Shadow considered his options.

Before surrendering his gift of wielding the powers of the rudenium stone, Shadow had discovered that Aries had left the realm and taken off to planet earth, though he could not fathom why Aries would have travelled to earth. Nevertheless, Shadow was grateful for Aries' departure. He hoped that her absence would buy him sufficient time to plan his next move carefully and regain needed strength.

"Beast!" Shadow yelled.

"Yes, master?" growled the beast.

"Drink this," Shadow held out his arm and a pail of liquid suddenly appeared in his palm. He set it down before the cherolith and the beast lapping it up eagerly.

"Lie down and rest for now. We'll reconvene later."

"As you wish, master," the beast complied, still slapping its tongue.

"Given that Aries has left the realm, I intend to summon Wizard Qarhan and seize his powers. Feel free to watch the show," Shadow said confidently. He had given this much thought. It was good that Aries had travelled to earth, although he remained ignorant of her plans for returning to the realm. Shadow believed that the key to conquering Aries would be the use of his vast wisdom to win his essences back from Aries when he saw her next. He had no idea when, but he was certain that she would return. Now more than ever Shadow wished that he could access the powers of the stone to spy on Aries. Shadow was conscious of his accrual of a null, and desperately hoped no other capable entity would become aware of this null. So far, he had one null accrual remaining. With Wizard Qarhan's powers, particularly the power of astral projection, Shadow could possibly project himself to wherever he so desired and seize Aries' powers without detection. Perhaps he could even trap Aries in another dream spell and subdue her before she fully transitioned into a lifeforce. Shadow settled on the conclusion that there was no way that Aries would ever gain enlightenment to such ancient knowledge as that of the Double Null Enchantment. In the unlikely event that she did, Aries would remain ignorant of the null that Shadow himself had incurred.

"Terrlashnavek Kabet Duminvalek funtamek," Shadow chanted. "Wizard Qarhan, come forth!"

CHAPTER 29
Svania: Wizard Qarhan

Wizard Qarhan and his team had congregated in the courtyard to verbally sort through their experience with Aries in the dungeon. They frantically discussed the 'so called' vision that Qarhan had shared with them, and although the team agreed that a meeting with Ziva was paramount, they were finding it difficult to process the wizard's recent inappropriate, out-of-character behavior. Their wizard had completely ghosted them, and they desperately contemplated what would happen next. Akello, being completely unaware of his wizard's astral projection abilities, had also been unaware that Qarhan had been present with him in spirit to witness Ziva's seduction of Aries. Hence the group's newfound admiration for Qarhan when he recited this incident, coyly referring to it as a vision. He'd even brought them to the cherolith's empty cell, to prove that his vision was indeed true, and the entity that might have possessed Ziva's body, had also captured Aries' cherolith.

The group consisted of Wizard Qarhan, Akello and his soldiers, the councilmen, Senya and Senya's maidens. They remained huddled together and drew comfort from each other.

"Qarhan, isn't there anything that you can do to help solve any of this?" Akello asked hoarsely.

"I—I'm not sure," Wizard Qarhan stuttered. "There seems to be great forces at play here—forces far greater and even more dangerous than anything I've ever witnessed," said Qarhan, suddenly regretting his tale about a vision.

"What do you mean?" Senya asked, frightened.

"Just as Ziva may no longer be the Ziva we knew, Aries may no longer be the Aries we once knew."

"Then who has she become?" Serena asked.

"I'm not quite sure. Though I was unable to interpret the strange words she had recited on that energy cloud, I did recognize the language," Qarhan explained to his highly attentive audience. "Aries had said *Dijimonek olosek*. These were the same words used by the Ziva entity when it had taken the cherolith—in my vision. Judging by her choice of language, Aries has either been possessed by a lifeforce, or is transforming into one."

"But how is this possible? Does this have something to do with Ziva?" Senya pressed, feeling frightened and resentful at the same time.

"I can't say for sure whether ..." Qarhan was struck mid-sentence by a sudden distant chant in which his name was continuously being repeated.

The group turned in unison to look in the direction of the sound. They could see nothing.

Terrlashnavek Kabet Duminvalek funtamek, Wizard Qarhan, come forth!

Terrlashnavek Kabet Duminvalek funtamek, Wizard Qarhan, come forth!

The group first searched each other's faces curiously until their gazes met with Qarhan's.

"Colleagues," Qarhan spoke ominously. "I fear that I am being summoned by a force that is far greater than me. I have no other option but to answer the call. Take great caution going forward—it appears that a greater force might be seeking to rule this realm."

"Wait, what?" Akello asked baffled.

"Akello, I will activate the portal for you to travel back to your people. Return to Asteria and warn our people of impending danger. You must not tarry..." Once again, Qarhan was stopped mid-sentence.

"Never mind this impending danger," said a familiar sounding voice. The group turned in unison to see Aries suspended just above ground level.

"Aries!" Senya exclaimed. "Are you the cause of all of this?" Senya spat furiously, but immediately jolted once the chant resumed.

Terrlashnavek Kabet Duminvalek funtamek, Wizard Qarhan, come forth!

"What's going on—how do you now have the ability to fly?" councilman five inquired nervously.

"I do not have time, so I'll try to shorten my explanation. If I'm to save this realm, you must promise to accept me as your leader. I need your spoken agreement. Do we have an agreement?" Aries asked.

"More trickery and lies!" Empress Senya grimaced bitterly. "How were you able to summon a flying cloud? You dissolved our kingdom's lifeforce so you could take over, didn't you?"

"If that's the case, then who's that summoning Wizard Qarhan, huh?" Aries retorted cleverly. "I suppose I'm the reason for this unknown being's presence in our realm, correct?" she asked pretending to be angry. She already knew the group remained baffled about the situation. They didn't know the whole story, and Empress Senya remained baffled. Aries intended to keep things this way. She planned to blame everything on the unknown entity that now possessed Ziva's body. "Empress Senya," Aries continued, her tone softer. "you'll have to set your foolish resentment aside to work with me."

"Have you forgotten just how much I know about you, huh? What you've done?" Senya sneered at Aries.

Terrlashnavek Kabet Duminvalek funtamek, Wizard Qarhan, come forth!

"Quickly, we do not have much time. The entity that has overcome Wizard Ziva—and I've perceived that you already are aware of this entity acquiring Ziva's body—is now summoning Wizard Qarhan to overtake his powers," Aries said, grateful for the save and inwardly gleeful that Shadow's chant had interrupted Senya's accusations.

"Let her tell us, who's behind the dissolution of our kingdom's lifeforce!" Senya spat knowingly. "Don't let her get away with another lie, please" Serena chimed in.

"I feel myself letting go—the pull from the summoning is too strong," Wizard Qarhan finally said desperately. "We have no other choice but to trust Aries. Please, my dear friends, I believe she's being truthful. For my sake, Akello, let us work with her! Such intrusive summoning by this unknown being can only mean trouble for me. For all of us," he pled.

The small gathering briefly exchanged disbelieving glances, but moments later they silently shrugged in agreement with Qarhan's plea.

"Very well. I take it we have an agreement," Aries smiled wickedly. "Only this time, my agreement with you is mutually beneficial. If we succeed, then we will have a great future ahead of us, with me as your leader. Do you understand?" she asked. The group responded with shrugs so subtle, that only Aries could detect them.

"I need your spoken agreement."

"As empress of Kingdom Svania, I grant you permission to lead my people," Senya muttered bitterly.

"Very good," said Aries. "I agree. I have somehow come into my own and I'm growing increasingly powerful. It is possible that I might be a lifeforce—or even an entity that is far more powerful than a lifeforce. Empress Senya believes that all of this might have started from one of my tricks, but believe me when I tell you this, these occurrences were bound to happen regardless of any trick. As you have witnessed, our situation is now dire. Senya, this is no time for lingering hate. A strange being has practically swallowed our entire lifeforce, stolen my cherolith, and now seeks to devour Qarhan so that it can destroy me. I have perceived it all. Am I making myself clear to you so far?"

"Yes," the group, sans Senya, replied in unison.

"The Nurians with all of their faculties," Aries continued, "had found a way to tele-travel to another planet which would have been to their demise if I hadn't made my way there to rescue them."

"They what?" Akello asked, shocked at the news.

"That's the least of our problems now," Aries continued. "Akello, what you should know is that after you stormed away from my cell earlier tonight, I had used my powers to unlink the bond Ziva had fashioned during his seduction spell—because that's what his seduction was about. He attempted to subdue me through use of a seduction spell." She paused for a moment and watched as realization and relief both swept across Akello's face.

Meanwhile Shadow's chant continued: *Terrlashnavek Kabet Duminvalek funtamek, Wizard Qarhan, come forth!*

"This brings me to my plan—Qarhan, are you still with me?" she continued.

"Yes," Qarhan gasped. "I'm trying to hang on with all my might, but the pull from the chant has started to overwhelm me. Whatever you have planned, you must do it quickly."

"Alright, try holding on for just a moment longer. You're being summoned by an entity known as the Shadow. I sensed him as soon as Ziva had bonded with me by giving me a portion of his essence as well as a portion of Shadow's essence."

"Wait, what?" the maidens exclaimed.

"Silence please, ladies," Akello commanded. He motioned for Aries to continue.

"Thank you, Akello," Aries continued. "When I unlinked the bond, I subdued both essences, and now I rule a part of Ziva and a part of Shadow." She paused momentarily.

"Just quickly tell us of your plan to beat this entity, please. What does this entity want from me?" Qarhan asked, his voice now raspy as he battled the forces of the summoning.

"Your gift of astral projection," Aries said.

"Qarhan possesses no such gift," Akello rebuffed.

"There are things that surpass the understanding of mortals," Qarhan cleverly counteracted. "Please, carry on Aries," Qarhan urged. There was no need for the group to suddenly learn about his secret. Now more than ever he was annoyed with himself for the senseless lies he'd told.

"Alright then, here goes. Wizard Qarhan, we'll work together to bring down the shadow ..."

"Shhh!" Senya suddenly whispered. "What if this shadow entity is listening in on us—what if he perceives our plan and Aries' presence here?"

"Great point, Senya," Aries said, smiling. "I'm happy to share that I had a vision of our Shadow entity surrendering his gift of wielding the power of a special stone he used to spy on people. He exchanged this gift for completely overtaking Ziva." Aries allowed a moment for the group to quickly process this information, then she continued. "Pick up your jaws my friends, I intend to perform my greatest maneuver yet. I intend to rid us of the great evil that has awoken in the Realm of Zannus. Wizard Qarhan, I command you to remain here with us until I'm through with my preparation," Aries said, seeing that Qarhan no longer had the strength to stave off the summoning on his own. She knew that the pain resulting from the simultaneous enchantments would be too great for Qarhan to bear, but it was necessary.

The chant reverberated: *Terrlashnavek Kabet Duminvalek funtamek, Wizard Qarhan, come forth!*

Qarhan wailed in agony but continued to stay put as the power of Aries' command compelled him to stay, while the power of Shadow's summoning pulled him away.

Aries swiftly hurled herself into Qarhan's arms and kissed him. "There," she said softly. "I need you to agree that we're now bonded."

"I agree that we're now bonded!" Qarhan wailed, entrusting his entire being into Aries' hands. He howled as the powerful forces pulled him in opposite directions. The group helplessly watched on in sheer dread.

"Now that we are bonded," Aries continued, "surrender unto me all of your gifts. My possession of your gifts is how I'll be able to successfully perform an astral loop, and then beat the Shadow," she explained. She marveled at her fierce wit. She had used her genius to rescue the Nurians and gain lordship over their kingdom through a covenant with Emperor Lunar. She carried the essences of hundreds of Nurian men within her. If she now gained access to all of Qarhan's powers, she had a sure chance of beating the Shadow and becoming ruler of Svania as well. Though, given the increasing immensity of her powers, she possibly may not have needed any leader's spoken authorization. Regardless, she would take no chances, especially given the fact that she was still unable to determine the true extent of her powers.

Wizard Qarhan obediently recited, "By the powers of all the ancient forces, I surrender to you, all of my powers." A force that was likened to that of a very strong wind was evident and could be seen tugging at Qarhan. His feet lifted above ground level as the winds picked him up and hoisted him off the ground.

"I perceive that Shadow pursues your powers, but I will counter his efforts and subdue him," Aries continued. "Essences of Ziva and Shadow, come forth!" she shouted. Immediately two entities unlatched themselves from her form. "You will go before me as we travel to Shadow," Aries commanded. "I now perceive him in the Kingdom of Octushi. You will release my cherolith from Shadow, and I will then reclaim my pet."

"Yes, mistress," the entities replied in unison.

"My cherolith will do as you command because you are indeed Shadow and Ziva, and you will command it's return to me. So, you will also retrieve from him, the rudenium stone."

"Yes, mistress."

"As for me," Aries uttered as she sat on the ground with her legs crossed, "I will be there to finish what Shadow has started. Wizard Qarhan, I now hereby release you unto Shadow," She commanded, closing her eyes and entering a deep meditation. As soon as Qarhan disappeared, Aries muttered something beneath her breath, immediately projecting herself from her body. Just as quickly as it had emerged, her projection quickly vanished alongside the Ziva and Shadow entities, leaving Aries' body behind. The astonished group hurried over to where Aries' body sat and stared at each other dumbfounded.

CHAPTER 30

Wizard Qarhan was the first to arrive at Kingdom Octushi, and he'd appeared before Shadow tattered and spent. The lengthy resistance to Shadow's summoning had severely weakened him, not to mention his surrender of his powers to Aries. Despite his depletion, he was intent on gaining Aries her prospect at the double-null enchantment against Shadow, whatever a double-null enchantment meant. There had been no time for Aries to explain this term to the group, but Qarhan hoped, for the sake of the kingdoms of Zannus Realm, that the enchantment would benefit them all.

"Ziva, why have you summoned me—what has been going on with you?" Qarhan gasped, slumping to the ground to alleviate his agony.

"Ziva is no more," Shadow boomed, his anger evident but controlled. The cherolith which sat a few yards away from them growled viciously but Qarhan was too weak to be terrified.

"What are you? What have you done with Ziva?" he asked breathlessly, refusing to look up and meet Shadow's gaze. Instead, he kept his eyes trained on the growling cherolith. Qarhan already knew that Ziva's body had been acquired, or better yet, possessed by Shadow. However, maintaining secrecy of this knowledge was probably his best play.

"I am Shadow. But something tells me you already know this," Shadow boomed, eyeing Qarhan pensively.

"Well so much for hiding that knowledge," Qarhan thought to himself. "Who or what told you that?" he asked Shadow anyway.

"Tell me something," Shadow continued, ignoring Qarhan's question, "what were you doing when I summoned you? Please explain the cause for such intolerable reluctance."

While Qarhan pondered on a logical reply, two ghostly entities, the Shadow and Ziva essences, suddenly appeared and hovered over to the cherolith.

"I release you from my service," the Shadow essence said to the beast. "Return to Aries, your rightful owner."

"Thank you," the beast replied, his response sending shockwaves throughout Shadow.

Qarhan too was shocked as he considered the beast to be even more ghastly now that it could speak. Qarhan desperately hoped that, should they triumph over Shadow, Aries would waste no time in muting her horrendous pet. He wondered why she'd chosen to pet a cherolith, but his thoughts were interrupted by Shadow's outcry.

"What sort of trickery is this?" Shadow exclaimed.

Once the essences had successfully released the cherolith from their service to Shadow, Aries, through her astral projection enchantment, quickly got to work.

"Arise, my dear pet," she whispered to the cherolith, "I welcome your return to your rightful place by my side. However, going forward you shall speak no more," the beast was immediately muted and could no longer speak. "Wait here right next to me," Aries said, patiently anticipating Shadow's response.

"There you are!" Shadow said, flashing Aries a cynical smile. "I wondered where you've been. Now you suddenly appear out of nowhere with the essences you've stolen from me. The trickster has performed her most endearing trick of all," Shadow shouted mockingly.

"This is my most endearing trick yet," Aries retorted, reminding herself that this was Shadow speaking, and not Ziva. This being,

Shadow, was far more sinister than anything or anyone she'd ever met.

"I beg to differ, my clever little trickster. You have managed to sneak into my domain and steal my beast," Shadow boomed, seemingly confident. "I could decimate you with just a snap of my fingers," he roared, his confidence terrifying Wizard Qarhan. There was no way that Aries could defeat such a menacing being. Qarhan was almost certain that soon they would all end up like Ziva—non-existent. There was just no escaping that bit of fact. The thought sent shivers down his spine.

"You must follow the rules, Shadow," Aries said nonchalantly. She observed Shadow's subtle shock at both her nonchalance and her knowledge of his name.

"So, you have indeed grown very powerful—I must admit that your knowledge of my name impresses me," Shadow hummed, his stare pensive.

"The rules, Shadow; you must play by the rules. First attend to your summoning before engaging me in a power match," Aries said coyly, her eyes dancing. "Go on then!"

Her indifference struck Shadow as alarming. Aries demonstrated no fear in facing an ancient lifeforce as himself. Shadow felt his confidence quickly waning. Despite all his glory, and all his wisdom, he'd been backed into a corner by Aries, whom he considered just a prospective lifeforce. He had to admit to himself that Aries was right. He had no choice but to attend to his summoning before anything else, thus carrying out his plan in front of a live audience. He hadn't anticipated seizing another person's powers while Aries and her minions watched.

"What is it that you seek, Aries? Why are we here in this moment?" Shadow asked, trying desperately to hide his sudden sense of desperation.

"I'll tell you everything you need to know—but only after you attend to your summoning. You're running out of time. You must either now release Qarhan from your summon, or carry out the goal of it," Aries said.

"I intend to carry out the goal of it," Shadow boomed angrily, frustrated that Aries had shown up at this moment. He suddenly wished he hadn't surrendered his powers to access the rudenium stone. But only by doing so could he have repressed Ziva and take over his body. Yet, if he hadn't done so, he could have spotted Aries return and anticipated her arrival at Octushi. She had shown up on his turf at the very moment he intended to usurp Qarhan's powers. Shadow subtly moved his palm motioning for his rudenium stone to appear in his palm. When it didn't, he grew perplexed. Shadow felt completely distracted and knew that the better play might be to release Qarhan until he could think things through more clearly, but he concluded that now was as good a time as any, to retrieve needed powers in order to immediately subdue Aries.

Meanwhile, Wizard Qarhan smiled to himself at his realization of the vast ingenuity of Aries' plot. She indeed was the greatest trickster of all. Until this very moment he'd been racking his brain in efforts of deciphering Aries' scheme. Trusting her with his powers had been a desperate, last-minute resort, until this very moment. He no longer doubted her ability to triumph over Shadow. This thought was enough to quicken his recovery.

"Do you think that you are any match for me?" Shadow challenged, despite the terrible feeling of unease that slowly crept up on him. Aries realized that he was stalling and disengaged from further conversation. She hoped that this move would guarantee her a straightforward victory, preventing her from having to expend the lives she'd borrowed from Lunar's men, and the powers she had borrowed from Wizard Qarhan. Aries gulped as she considered the hundreds of borrowed essences she now carried within her. She observed Shadow's hesitation at seizing Qarhan's gifts. She suddenly perceived his awareness of the null he'd accrued, but she couldn't read his thoughts to know whether Shadow had started to decipher her knowledge about the accrual. Had he deciphered why she had arrived there in the exact moment of the summoning? Had he figured out her intentions of luring him into a second null accrual? How much wiser it would have been for Shadow to postpone his plan of greed and deceit.

"How desperate you must be to have shown up here as my spectator," Shadow finally said. "Qarhan!" he roared, "By the forces of the great force-fields, I command that you surrender all your powers to me!" he boomed despite his uncertainties surrounding Aries' intentions.

Aries breathed a sigh of relief which eased Wizard Qarhan's mind.

"But I'm already bonded to Aries—only she may command me," Qarhan explained boldly, faking empathy towards Shadow.

"What?" Shadow was confounded.

"I've already surrendered my powers to Aries ..."

"I heard you!" Shadow grimaced, cutting him off. "Then you must die, Qarhan," Shadow roared, his palms suddenly alighting. Just as he begun to amass a thunder ball to strike Qarhan, Aries stopped him.

"Shadow, I challenge you to the double null enchantment," she exclaimed.

The thunder ball gradually dissipated from Shadow's palms as he complied with the ancient law of the force-fields. Anger and frustration stirred within him. Though aware of this possible outcome, he'd been caught off guard and this distracted him. He hadn't been used to such distractions. On the one hand he was certain of one null but hadn't been able to think things through wisely.

"State your charges," he said, swallowing his feelings and kneeling before Aries who had now glided over to him. In that moment he fully realized his devastating error.

"Your first null," begun Aries, "was your failure at seizing my gift of foresight. I did not possess all the powers at the time you attempted to seize them from me. Do you honor this stated null?" she asked confidently.

"I honor the null," Shadow said, defeated.

"Your second null was your failure to seize all of Qarhan's powers. When you attempted the seizure, Wizard Qarhan had already been bonded to me and had surrendered all of his powers to me. Do you honor this null?"

"I do," Shadow said, his grandeur melting away into the nothingness to which he would be banished. This was the null he had missed. Had he utilized more wisdom, he could have avoided this predicament. He blamed Ziva for the predicament, but he blamed himself for merging with Ziva in the first place. Had it not been for his desire to assume human form—had it not been for his greed…

"Your third null," Aries continued, disrupting Shadow from his thoughts, "was your failure to seize my cherolith," Aries paused purposefully.

She had seen the smile flicker across Qarhan's face. She could also tell that Qarhan was growing increasingly fascinated by the scene that unfolded. She quickly glanced over at her cherolith who sat easily licking it's paws close to where Shadow knelt.

"What a witch!" Shadow thought to himself. "Only two nulls were needed."

"Shadow, do you honor these three nulls?" Aries asked.

"This is overkill, but yes, I do." Shadow agreed, devastated that his awakening had been so short-lived. His time had come to an end. His reign as lifeforce had ended just as quickly as it had begun.

"Shadow, you have honored the nulls that I have brought against you. I am hereby sanctioned to enforce the double null enchantment, which will be used to have you return Ziva to us at once. You will then be banished to your pre-existence with no possibility of returning," Aries commanded. "Terrlashnavek Kabet Duminvalek funtamek, Ziva!" she recited.

"Terrlashnavek Kabet Terrnalishu noctek sperroshes, Shadow," she concluded, bidding Ziva to come forth, and Shadow to disperse.

As Shadow's silhouette emerged from Ziva's body, Ziva capsized to the ground and convulsed. Shadow hovered over Ziva's body briefly before dispersing into thin air.

"You are the trickiest genius of them all!" Qarhan applauded Aries.

"We're almost out of time!" Aries replied, quickly gliding over to Qarhan. "You must help me forge a path back to my kingdom," Aries said.

"Here, boy!" Qarhan whistled for the cherolith to join them. Once the beast and Ziva were secured in their arms, Qarhan locked lips with Aries as she returned Qarhan's powers back to him. A powerful gust of wind engulfed and swept them up into an unseen path back to the kingdom of Svania.

EPILOGUE

Zannus Realm forms the Zannusian Pyramid, which comprises four kingdoms. Kingdoms Asteria, Svania and Octushi form the base of this pyramidal monarchy, while the fourth Kingdom, Nuria, referred to as the light of the realm, sits at the realm's apex. It is through the light of this realm that a new empress, and lifeforce, Aries, addresses the realm and watches over the people of the kingdoms of Zannus. Aries has fully acclimated to her powers, and the people of all three kingdoms are happy with her reign thus far. The Nurians, with their great intellect are finally content at living freely. They happily provide the realm with crucial technological advancements. They no longer live in fear of the Asterians.

Aries has returned the lives she had borrowed from Nuria, and Ziva is particularly happy at his freedom to carry on as wizard despite the collapse of the water-force. Aries had performed a ritual to untether from her, the Shadow essence and the Ziva essence which she had successfully confiscated. She had dispensed both essences into Ziva to preserve his immortality. Though Ziva now carries a little of Shadow within him, the people of Zannus Realm are happy to have the real Ziva back. Aries has complete confidence that the Shadow essence she's granted Ziva will remain faithful to Ziva. Ziva, with the essence of the Shadow lifeforce within him, can now teleport. So, he collaborates efforts with Wizard Qarhan, under the oversight of Empress Aries. Wizard Qarhan admits in jest, that he was once jealous of Wizard Ziva. The two occasionally share laughs at past conflicts between them.

Aries' powers have not developed to the all-seeing levels she had hoped for, but she is happy that her powers have grown enough to grant her the status of lifeforce of the realm. Aries finds that her efforts at peeking at things outside of Zannus Realm often depletes her powers and severely weakens her gift of foresight. Though she can see things beyond the realm, she often opted not to, but instead, directed her focus at maintaining a peaceful and joyful realm.

Akello, no longer chief, continues his pursuit of his parents' forgiveness, though his father strongly believes that the power-shift within Zannus realm was caused by Akello's blasphemy. Senya remains resentful of the power-shift. She hates that Akello and herself are no longer leaders and that Wizard Ziva and Wizard Qarhan both function as the realm's two executive leaders under the new Empress Aries. Akello is content with the privilege of having fallen in love with a great lifeforce, and now pursues Serena who was once Senya's lead maiden. Qarhan, who was once Akello's wizard, reminisces with the once councilmen, about the kisses he had shared with Aries. Both Akello and Qarhan often chuckle together at this bit of fact.

Senya has lost her reign and secretly begrudges Aries. She completely despises the new empress but manages to keep this hatred hidden. For now.

Aries marvels at her own power. She has finally gotten what she'd always dreamed of—power over the kingdoms of Zannus realm. She secretly keeps a special eye on Senya as she remains well aware of the woman's contempt for her. No telling when another lifeforce might appear out of nowhere again and this time challenge Aries' reign as Empress of the Kingdoms of Zannus Realm.

<u>Ancient Language of Zannusian Lifeforces: Interpretation</u>

Selavimiyk, cherolith: You now serve me, cherolith.
Selavimiyk, sperroseh: You serve me spirit
Selavimiyk etyl evonomek: You all shall serve me
Malevomiyk, vilenosyske actek: I serve no one, I am ruler by myself

**Malevomiyk vilenosyske actek,
Selavimiyk unyit, o'te
sperrosehes vai o'te onomekes
vai evonomek:** I serve no one, I am ruler alone of spirits and of all men and of all.

Selavimiyk yunsek, Shadow: You will serve me, Shadow.
Duminvalek funtamek: Come forth
Terrlashnavek Kabet: I bid you
Dijimonek olosek: Transport us
Ven: Enter
Selavimiyk: Serve me
Selavu: Serve you
Oslavo terrselavu: Master, I serve you
Ay Miyk: To me
Suspehes: Speak
Mustrak: Beast
Terrnalishu noctek: I banish you into nothingness